Through Her Eyes

Olamide Adejola

Thank you for your Support
OA 03/2022

Chicago | Ontario | Lagos

Through Her Eyes© Olamide Adejola

7th Seal Advantage Publishing, LLC

This Book and other publications by the author are available at all major bookstores and book outlets nationwide.

ISBN: 978-1-7377864-3-6

Cover Design: MidoDezines

www.7thsealadvantage.com

DEDICATION

To that single parent who feels lonely and without help…

To those parents with feelings of regret for sending their child to be raised by another person…

And to those children and young adults who are scared, living with someone other than their parents.

CONTENTS

ACKNOWLEDGEMENTS

Through Her Eyes is a metamorphized product of a long-term process of decades. Firstly, I praise God for making this a possibility, especially for the gift of men He has made available in making the completion of the project a success. My gratitude goes to the man in my life - my love and best friend, Pastor Rotimi Adejola, who has remained the great supporter of my life dreams and my cheer leader.

I salute and appreciate my Spiritual mother, Rev. Dr. Mrs. Adesola Babalola, who saw the significance of this book even before I did. The light you provided inspired me to pursue the project beyond me, for others to learn and benefit from my past ordeal.

To my children, parents, siblings, and other family members who have been a source of encouragement and support in this process; I say thank you all. To my dear friends who saw how impactful this story is to every parent, you are another source of energy that kept me going then and even now in the pursuit of destiny matters.

Finally, I say a big thank you to my editor, publishing team for their never-ending hard work. Without Deaconess Sheri Asuoha in particular, I doubt if this project would have seen any daylight – God will surely send you help at the appropriate time when needed.

For now

We see through a mirror.

Darkly.

But then… face to face.

For now I know only in part.

But then shall I know

Even as also

I am known.

-1 Corinthians 13:12-

FOREWORD

As we read through this book, two scriptures came to light. The first is Psalm 40:3, NKJV and it reads, "He has put a new song in my mouth- Praise to our God; Many will see it and fear And will trust in the LORD." The other that came to my mind is John 1:46, NKJV that says, "…And Nathanael said to him, "Can anything good come out of Nazareth?" Philip said to him, "Come and see."

The book, "Through Her Eyes" is one of the most down to earth books we've read in these recent days. It is full of stories of redemption. If you ever wondered how God could take someone from nothing to something, this book will definitely give you an idea.

Over the years, we've interacted with people who share stories similar to the mother and daughter described in this book. We found that people seldom live through the bitterness that such experiences inflict upon them. Sadly, many never see their chance to rise again. But, the stories of the main characters in this book tell us something better. Their stories show us what hope lies ahead for anyone who is willing to put their trust in God and partner with the people God has ordained to help them in life. The same is true for the author of this book. Her story is one we must all learn from and rejoice in. Her story is the story of victory in Christ Jesus!

Auntie, as we normally call her, has been an amazing member of our church family. She is major proof of our calling to apostleship. More importantly, she is a proof of the transforming power of the gospel. Little wonder she has been able to turn ashes to beauty and her mourning into dancing. The testimony of her life and others that have crossed her path in destiny, bring the Biblical testimonies we have read about beyond the limelight and into reality.

It's our pleasure to see her being changed from glory to glory and summoning the courage to put the most intimate pieces of her testimony into story form. Her creativity and passion for delivering such a timely message for today's families is more than commendable.

Beloved, whether you are a young person who desires not to make critical mistakes… a young chap wondering what can come of your mess… a single parent… or someone just trying to find their faith, we recommend this book for you and we assure you that you will be blessed as you read it.

-Rev. & Rev. Dr. 'Sola Babalola,

Pastors of Kingdom Pathway Church

I.

YOU ARE NOT JOSEPH

"My story is the story of Joseph," she would say calmly, and with all certitude. Mommy always boasted of Joseph's trials and of the tribulations he endured as if they were her own. They were not. "He was treated and traded like a slave… and by his own brothers!" she reminded us. "I, too, came from another country," she would always say. "I was accused of things that were not true. There were times I was punished when I did nothing wrong." You could see the story at play in her mind. It made me sick. Sometimes, literally.

"Like Joseph, I was separated from my father who loved me dearly," she smiled and winked at my brother, of course. Then she looked at me. "I did not know what my future would hold. The very people who I trusted as family… the people my parents trusted…" She always stopped there as if there was some kind of guardsman or a monster who stood at the tip of her tongue threatening to seize her tongue, should she bear another word.

Then, you would see her perk up as if she just remembered she knew a secret or some kind of code that gave her access to the back channels of a better story.

"No one could stop God's plan for my life," she would grin, shoulders back. "What hell meant for my downfall, God used to elevate me. See me now!" On one of such days, she started dancing. I felt like puking. Out of the corner of my eye, I saw my oldest brother, Thomas, grinning. I frowned. Usually, he looked like he was with me on this. But he seemed pleased with our mother's ridiculous dramatics. "I am just like Joseph."

"Hey! Josephina!" My other brother, Daniel, laughed as he danced along. He thought he was such a clever comedian. He was not. My mom thought he was, though. She would smile proudly, her face perfectly made, just as her life was, as she danced next to her perfect sons.

Every time Mommy came to tell us her Joseph story, I kept quiet. I even kept my body language quiet. Should I have given her the side eye I thought she deserved, she would have sounded me across the face. I couldn't bring myself to pretend to be interested either, though. Maybe because I knew too much about Joseph's story. It was nothing like the story of this woman that stood before my eyes. She looked nothing like a person who life had done wrong.

My mother was a minister in our church. A prophetess. And the one everyone liked. They came to her for business advice, medical advice and every kind of advice. I guess that's why she thought she knew everything. Maybe she did know a lot. But she definitely did not know me.

I knew all about the 'Joseph' she claimed to be like because my mother made my brothers and I attend Sunday School, every single Sunday, and children's church on Wednesdays. What I knew most about Joseph was that he was not the only son of Jacob, though he wanted to act like it. Jacob had 12 sons, each with his own character and story to tell. But I also knew what most church kids my age did not know and that was that Jacob had a daughter. Her name was Dinah. They never taught us about Dinah in Sunday School. People rarely speak of her story, much like they seldom speak of mine. I guess because they were ashamed of her and the problem she seemed to cause just for existing. I only learned about her by accident. But the day I learned about her, it changed my life.

It was my brother's fault, actually. We were supposed to be looking for a memory verse that one of our Sunday School teachers had given us when we stumbled across her tragedy in Genesis 34. I wasn't the best reader at the time, but I remember seeing Daniel's eyes widen in both confusion and disbelief- two things I thought were not supposed to happen when you read the word of God.

"What is it? What does it say?" I whined eagerly, welcoming the healthy distraction from memorizing scripture. I was about seven or eight years old at the time. He was hesitant to tell me anything and that further piqued my curiosity. "Either tell me our memory verse or tell me what you're reading. What's the big deal?" I asked, annoyed but interested.

Finally, he answered, "Did you know Jacob had a daughter?" *Jacob? Abraham's Seed that we sing about? Father of the 12 tribes… the 12 sons, there was a girl, too?* "He did?" I asked excitedly. "Let me see!" Daniel looked at it again. "Nope." He said firmly. "It's too mature for your age." What did Daniel know about maturity? Did he not just get in trouble for making spitballs in class at his age? It was the Bible. The same one they told us to read every day. How bad could her story be?

"Let me see! Let me see!" I shouted, pulling his arm as I reached desperately for his Bible as if we were not in a church and there weren't 50 other Bibles laying around that I could have taken. One of our Sunday School teachers came along eventually. "What's going on, you two?" she asked, her kindness and concern obvious. Church could be long and draining, especially when your mom is a minister and keeps you there all day. But there were three things I always liked: my friends, praise and worship time, and my Sunday school teachers, well, most of them. Mom was a Sunday School teacher, too. I preferred getting my lectures from her at home. This teacher was one of my favorites because she was always telling us crazy Bible secrets and brought the best snacks. Daniel answered her,

"I am trying to tell Mercy this Bible story is way too mature for her. But I have a question too, Auntie…"

"Yes, what is it?" she smiled. She was delighted we were fighting about wanting to read the Bible and not something silly. But her countenance changed when my brother asked his question. "What is rape?" I watched Auntie's smile slowly melt into something more suitable for the occasion.

That's when I first learned Dinah's story. I was so young, I didn't understand it then, but her story always stayed with me. Genesis 34, I would tell myself. Years later, Genesis 34 still rang aloud in my mind and when I turned 10, I looked it up again on my own. Unlike my brother, I wasn't triggered by the "rape" part. I got angry about everything else. Her story pierced my heart because it was like she didn't have a voice. At all. All the things she was going through with the guy who hurt her, then wanted to marry her, and her brothers and her dad getting so mad at everyone… the war. And she was just there, and I never saw where she said anything. That resonated with me, deeply.

For years, I had something to say… and could not. In church, I watched, for years, as Daniel marched and stomped around, reciting scriptures, and saying whatever was on his mind. It took years, past the normal age of doing so, for me to finally be able to talk because of my tracheal situation. I couldn't march and stomp around like Daniel, or Dinah's brothers because I had to lug around machines, a tank of oxygen and a ton of tubes just to leave the house.

I shouldn't complain. The day finally came when I didn't have to carry around my breathing machine or my suction machine or the 0_2 tank or a nurse just to go out in public, and for that I was truly grateful. The second I knew I could talk, that day, I said EVERYTHING. No one had to beg me to grab a mic or sing a song or recite a scripture. I didn't care who was watching when I danced because I remembered there was a time I could not. People would watch and dance and smile along with me.

But sometimes, when church was over, I would go home, or to school, and I still felt like I couldn't dance or talk, and if I tried, like Dinah, my voice might get lost somewhere in translation. I felt like that for years. And the older and healthier I grew, it was as if the testimony of my healing was the end of any story people would listen to about me. I kind of felt like Dinah in that way. Like after the war and trouble her brother got into for her, everyone was just tired and there was nothing left to say, or no other blessings were on the way.

Like Dinah, I, too, am the only daughter of my mother and father. I was never raped (I cringed when I finally found out what that meant), but at an early age, I knew the feeling of losing all control over your life. I had the scars and hospital bills to prove that I, like Dinah, suffered unspeakably. And that's why I hated my mother's "Joseph" rant the most. She never truly suffered. She talked as if she had some grand overcoming because of one plane trip to Canada and a car ride to the States. She forgets we know her parents.

Her parents-my grandparents-were and still are very well off. They are among the elite in Ilésà and among the most well-to-do in Lagos, both cities in Nigeria. Both my grandparents always had jobs, fancy ones and they made money even while many in their city were struggling to make ends meet. They had enough money to help others. They sent their daughter off to school overseas just like all the rich African parents do. Her parents loved her and understood her.

In fact, if you ask me, Grandpa still spoils her to this very day. Mommy was always well-liked by everyone and still is. She was never a burden, like I always felt, especially when I was younger. Mommy was always healthy. Ironically, she is a doctor. It seemed the only downside to her life was having me, a sick child. But she even knew how to make my life one of her great assets, no matter how it affected me.

"Mercy, are you even listening?" I snapped back to reality. I forgot she was still talking. "Yes, Mommy, please continue." I tried to look as interested as my 12-year-old heart could stand. "Ah, are you okay? Continue ke? What did I even say just now?" I could see my brothers snickering in the corner of my eye. "I was listening, Mommy," Daniel, my older brother offered, as if anybody asked him.

"Shut up!" I yelled at him.

"Who do you think you're talking to, little girl?" he snarled.

"I'm talking to you!" I responded as firmly as I planned to plant my fist into his cheek. I'd been itching to get my hands on his smug, annoying face since we got home from school. I was ready to fight Thomas too, if he tried to stop me.

"Enough! Mercy, calm down before you stress yourself out!" Mommy commanded effectively enough for us to hold fire. "I am telling you all these because I heard what happened in school today. Mercy, you know you can always tell the teacher. But also, if you feel like someone is not treating you right, or something is not fair, I just want you to remember, Joseph had a similar story… just look, I…"

"Enough, Mommy, please! You don't know anything about my story. My story is nothing like yours. You think you know everything but…" a cough interrupted me. "You think… you think…"

"Mercy! Honey, are you okay?"

"I'm fine," I managed to say. I felt a bit dizzy, but I fought it. I found my seat as I adjusted to a familiar feeling.

"Mercy, is this what caused your issue at school today? Have you been feeling sick?" I did not reply to her. I needed my energy for something else.

"I told you she was acting funny on the bus the other day, Mommy. I told you! I tried to ask if she was okay, but she was being so mean." I didn't have time to respond to Daniel's absurd and distorted sense of reality.

God, when will this end? I thought to myself.

Soon. I looked up. No one was there but Daniel and Mommy. Thomas, our oldest brother must have gone to get Dad. I guess that was the first time I truly heard God.

I don't remember much of anything else that happened that day. It was the next day by the time I opened my eyes and saw light again. Mommy and Daddy were there looking at me.

"Finally, my princess is awake," Daddy smiled. I smiled too. I saw Mommy drawing closer. I was sure she would give me a kiss on the forehead and ask how I was feeling. But no. She looked into my eyes. "I hope you see what I mean. You can't just keep getting all worked up like that. You have to relax. God is healing you; you know that. Just relax and communicate. Trust God. He will help you just like He helped me. You know my story. Whenever I feel like things are not working, I just remember Joseph..." She could not be serious. Was she for real? I had never argued with my mother before. I did not have the energy to raise my voice or argue with anyone. But I made the energy. That day, as I laid in that hospital bed, everything changed.

"Mommy, stop," I commanded as loudly as I could, though I think I only made it just above a whisper. "Just stop. Please. You are not Joseph. You are just an immigrant ..." I expected her to interrupt me by now. Maybe she could not hear me. Or maybe she wanted to interject, but my dad intercepted. If so, go Dad!

I was too weak to lift my head to read her facial expression. I could not tell how mad she was. But the silence in the room proved she heard me and heard me well. So, I kept going. She needed to know the truth. She couldn't flog me while I was laying, sick in a hospital bed. Could she? It didn't matter. She could not make me feel any worse than I already did. "So what if you think you are special like Joseph? Stop bragging it to us. Didn't you learn anything from the story? How much his brothers hated him because he only talked about himself. Everybody can't be their father's favorite. Some of us have real problems we didn't cause by ourselves. You cry because you think you are like Joseph. You don't know suffering. You don't know what it's like to feel like..." It hurt my throat to push the words out. "Dinah... Nobody talks about Dinah."

II.

YOU ARE NOT DINAH

I felt my husband's hand cover my own, gently, but firmly. He didn't want me to respond. What would I have said? "Little girl. The child that I pushed out and labored and prayed and cried over almost every day for more than 12 years. It's you who knows nothing because I protected you in ways my family could not protect me."

I felt a tear, warm, making its way down my cheek until it burned at the corner of my lip. It wasn't her words that stung me. It was the contempt. The resentment. The judgement that rang loudly in her whisper of a voice.

I think I went into shock that day. I must have been in shock because I don't remember anything I was feeling before anger slowly began to take over my body. My husband squeezed my hand more firmly. He must have felt the anger taking over. He did his best to help me stop the rage in its tracks, but he was only partially successful. I shook his hand from mine. I took a breath in through my nostrils and let the remainder of the air out through my clenched teeth, then I walked briskly out of the room before the anger took its true form- a form that stood somewhere between hurt and despondency. I needed time.

I was sitting in the lounge, tea in hand, staring out the hospital window when my husband, Simi, sat before me. I couldn't bring myself to make eye contact with him. Not yet.

"She's just upset. She is growing up," he reasoned. "She just wants her healing to be complete. Please, my dear. Don't take it personally."

"Her healing is complete in Jesus' name." That prophecy left my lips seamlessly. I truly believed it. I did not feel like saying much of anything, but no matter how I felt, I was still a prophetess, a minister of the true and living God and He compelled me to say it.

"Amen," my husband agreed. I sipped my tea as I continued

to gaze into the sunset.

"Honey, I know you only want what is best for her. For all of them. She will know that, too, with time," he encouraged.

"Hmm," was the only response I could muster.

Simi smiled. I felt his eyes glistening about my face, just waiting for me to push my feelings aside and hear him clearly. I couldn't see him as I kept my eyes fixed on the nature scene that stared back at me through the hospital café window, but I knew he was smiling.

"Lizzy, darling, remember when we went through something like this with Thomas a few years back? He was just so angry. I think he gets that anger from you." I almost grinned but I held back. I wasn't ready to face hope. "But you understood with him," he continued. "Honey, you have been through this before and you overcame it," he asserted.

"It didn't feel like this," I retorted. "It wasn't painful." I was ready to look at Simi now. "This is different. This hurts." And finally, I let the remainder of the tears I'd been holding hostage roll down my cheeks. "It's so painful," I went on. "It's like she blames me for her pains… her ailment. She thinks it's my fault… and honestly, she is right. She's right. It was my womb, my angry, violent, abused womb…" By now, the tears had taken over.

My husband looked at me both tenderly and with a fearless, fatherly rebuke, "Don't say that, Woman of God. We don't talk like that. God does not make any mistakes. There is nothing wrong with you. There is nothing wrong with our daughter. Mercy is a miracle and a testament to God's goodness to us. Every day, her life declares that God indeed is a Healer. You know that." I didn't respond. "I said you know that." he said, no longer smiling. He needed to know that I knew. Mercy's life, our miracle and our position before the Lord depended on that.

"I know. I know. It's just that Thomas being angry made sense, Simi. Thomas suffered. He knew me before I was anyone's pastor. He knew me as just a single mom without a penny to my name. He has seen me at my lowest since before he was old enough to talk in complete sentences. Thomas would have every right to blame me for a hard life, but he does not. He was angry, yes, but he didn't blame everything on me. He understood with me. But Mercy and Daniel have had it very easy. We truly gave them the best of ourselves. I can even understand Daniel being mad if he wanted to be because he sacrificed a lot while we were working, building, schooling and when we were finally home, we were taking care of Mercy. We were at the hospital with her day in and day out. He missed out on so much- holidays, after school activities because we were always at the hospital with her. But Simi, I try to do everything for Mercy. We sacrificed everything for her. Yes, it can't be easy having medical challenges, but look at how far God has brought her! Look at the testimonies! Look at everything I sacrificed- we sacrificed. There's never been a time she wakes up and we are not there."

"Hmm! I think this is the longest you've ever not been in that hospital room with her." Simi offered.

"Why would she say that to me? How could she talk to me like that? I love my baby girl. Why does she hate me? Why, Simi? Why?" I hoped to find the answer in his eyes as I always did. He was quiet as expected. Simi was always quiet. But he let his eyes do the talking. I searched them for reassurance or hope at the very least. Without words, he whispered, gently, what I needed to hear. His eyes told me I knew better. I sighed in relief.

"There is so much Mercy does not know," he finally said.

"And for good reason," I reminded him. "She does not need

to know," I insisted. "It's our job to protect her from such burdens." We were her parents. I stirred my tea, small. "It's all in the past, anyway," I justified.

As I twirled the plastic spoon in my tea again, I lulled myself down memory lane.

The first time I met Simi was fourteen years ago at a local café, after only two surprisingly long phone calls that I never even planned to take.

"I don't have time for booty calls. That point in my life is over," I shot at him sharply. He looked at me with sheer innocence. He didn't seem naïve or inexperienced, he seemed… incorruptible. "Booty call, Ma? I don't understand." He said as if I was speaking to him in an unfamiliar tongue.

"Don't play dumb. You know what 'booty' is. Or are you saying you don't want any?" I gazed into his eyes searching for the weakness I knew must be there. That weakness that was in every man.

"Yes, I know what it is and…" His eyes excused themselves

from mine and made their way casually about my body… first, sampling my intentionally unmade face… then they took a deep dive into my dimples as if skinny-dipping. They came out, moved down my neck and towards my arms. I clenched my cuffs as his eyes briefly attended to my roughly three-week-old manicure. He grinned before he went any deeper or further, politely returning his eyes back to mine. "Yes," he finished as he cleared his throat. "…of course, I will want it eventually. And I will have it." He said it firmly and I believed him so much so that it put a shiver down my spine. *This man is bold*, I thought to myself.

"But all that comes after marriage," he snapped me right out of my daydream. "Right now," he continued, "…we take time to get to know ourselves. Tell me about yourself," he asked, caringly and with the most sincere interest I think I had ever experienced in my life. It caught me off guard.

I cleared my throat of slight embarrassment. Or maybe it was shyness. Neither of those were something I typically felt, but it occurred to me just then that he wanted me to tell him about myself when the truth was… I'd lost myself years ago.

I tried to remember the last time I truly knew who I was. I

could only recall the familiarly hot day that I boarded the plane with my auntie in Ikeja. On the way to the airport, we drove hours for what should have been a drive of a few minutes because of horrible traffic, but I didn't feel it because my body was so full of excitement. I had never been on a plane before. I still had my innocence and all the hope in the world. I was happy. I was myself.

When I met Simi, I was two years into recovering from four long and messy years of what I call a "pseudo-marriage." The relationship was physically painful. I had more scars than I cared to count to prove it. The wounds Akin left on my life were deep. I had taken about two years to heal and because of him and everything he took from me, the pain he caused, I vowed never to love again. That was the plan. But God had other plans. He wanted me to want what I longed in my heart to hate.

A few months after I'd gotten myself back into church, one evening, just a few days to my 30th birthday, I had taken off my church clothes and hung them neatly away. I removed my make up. I looked in the mirror and realized I was naked. I began to cry. I was not alone in the house. But I felt so lonely, it ached. "No, God, it hurts to be like this. Why am I so alone?" I cried to God. "I am tired of being by myself. I don't want a boyfriend." I was talking to God but suddenly, I felt something, like another entity. *They'll only hurt you. They'll use you and leave you. You're safer alone. In fact, who would have you? At your age, and in your condition… you come with baggage.* It was only with the word "baggage" that I snapped out of it. My son was not baggage. Thomas was the most beautiful part of me. The little of the Holy Ghost I had at the time helped me to reject every demonically arranged thought that wanted to invade my heart. It was then I was first introduced to a new phase of my life… this unfamiliar side… the anointing. So, I did what I could have only done by the anointing at that tender time of life, and I prophesied to myself. "I am the daughter of the King. I deserve love. No more boyfriends. This time next year, I will have a fiancé. I want the husband God has for me." I thought I was praying. Once the anointing waned, it all seemed like a silly, desperate prayer.

One time, my friend had introduced me to this guy, handsome and well-to-do "Christian". I had fixed myself up and was smiling from ear to ear when we finally met in person. He took one look at me and said, "I'm sorry, I can't. Your skin. You're just too light." I was too light. My smile widened all the more until I began to laugh hysterically as I walked away. I had so much confidence in myself, his words didn't faze me one bit. At that time, I had more confidence in me than I did in Christ. I moved on as I knew that I could and dated a few more times to no avail. I met Akin back in the States. We met in school while I was pursuing my nursing degree.

"Hello, Beautiful!" he said as he set eyes on me. He promised me the moon and it wasn't long before we moved in together. I was so delighted to tell my parents. I finally found the man I thought would love me the rest of my life. I never knew there was a woman somewhere who felt the exactly as I did about the same man I was in love with. He started being away more and every time I questioned him, it became a fight. A condescending fight. He would dangle papers in front of me. He wanted me to do things… unspeakable things and if I could not deliver or refused, he threatened to have me deported. Despite the challenges we were having, I became pregnant and what should have been the most exciting time of my life became filled with terror.

He introduced me to a lady… a lady who could 'help' me. My husband had been here much longer than I. He was the only person I could trust about many things. We did not have insurance, so he told me to have my baby using the lady's name. I thank God Almighty for the little measure of the Holy Spirit I had that wouldn't allow me to go through with it. I later learned he had plans to replace me and rob me of my identity, making it impossible for me to ever get my papers. But me saying no angered him greatly. He made life hell for me up to the day I gave birth and beyond.

The next time I ever felt joy was when I finally gave birth to our beautiful, bouncing baby boy. Thank God he took after me. "Hmm," I remember Akin commenting at the hospital, "Are you sure he's even mine?" The audacity. I put up with many more insults for many more nights. The insults became more and more physical by the day.

When I was tired enough, I left. Or, at least, I tried to. I was technically undocumented, so my options were limited. I also had Thomas, my baby. My health was troubling me as well. I had no family that I knew of in America at the time and my family in Canada was completely out of the question. One night, things got so bad, I ran to the only place I could think of- his father's house.

My father-in-law, unlike his son, was a kind and gentle man. "Thank you, Baba mí. I didn't know where else to go," I said.

"It's okay, my daughter. You gave me my first grandson. You are always welcome here." I was safe there- until one day, there was a knock at the door. I was in the other room when my father-in-law came to get me. "Akin is here for you," my father-in-law informed me. He looked as troubled as I did. "Where is she?" I heard Akin bellow. I held my breath and my son tight.

Akin looked at me and somehow, I knew whatever he wanted to say was going to cause me pain. "We just have to go to court," he announced. No greeting. "For immigration. It's to help with your papers. If you don't come, you'll be in trouble," he said. I was not too familiar with the immigration laws in the United States. I only ever knew what he told me. I decided I had no choice. He had already put me through so much, what worse could happen? I was scared. "I will come with you people," my father-in-law offered.

"No!" Akin ordered firmly. "They won't let you in, Daddy. Only me and Liz can go."

"You might need help with Thomas. I will come and just be around in case. I won't take no for an answer." He began to gather himself and help pack Thomas' diaper bag. Akin rolled his eyes, "We need to go now."

"We'll ride with Daddy, then," I informed Akin.

"Hmm, that's fine since you still have the mind of a schoolgirl and need a daddy to help you."

I ignored his comments and Thomas and I followed Akin to the immigration office located in the courthouse. Daddy stayed outside while I waited with Thomas in his stroller at Akin's side. The wait was cold. We did not speak. They eventually called us back. Was this really the interview? Was he going to finally help me get my papers and let me go? We had done all the paperwork and I had given him every cent I made towards it for all the fees. My heart went from fearful to excited, especially seeing happy couples come out of the office after their interviews. We got into the office, and I smiled warmly at the officer who smiled back as he doted over our baby. "What's his name?" the officer smiled. "Thomas," I responded. Akin rolled his eyes, irritated by the small talk. Eventually the officer began with his line of questions. "How long have you two been married?"

"Nearly four years," I replied. "We met in school, at the community college." I offered.

"Oh nice," the officer smiled.

"I want her deported," Akin announced unsolicited. He caught me completely off guard and I froze. The officer was just as taken aback as I was. "I beg your pardon," he asked to be sure he heard what he heard. "She is illegal. I married her, yes, but I didn't know her status. She is a liar. She is cheating the system".

"But this is your wife." The officer was still puzzled.

"I don't care," he replied. I sat quietly, confused and ashamed, but not totally surprised. The officer looked at me and back at him. "You have a child together. This your child? Thomas, is it?" He inquired, still perplexed.

"I do not care. I don't want to continue the filing process, please. I want her out of the States".

The officer looked at my baby then at me. I was scared. Panic and fear enveloped my face... my heart. The immigration officer signaled me towards the door. "Ma'am," he looked me directly in the eye. I could sense Akin's smug grin as the officer moved towards me. I braced myself. I didn't know if I should expect handcuffs. A part of me even wanted to run. But how could I run with Thomas and his stroller and diaper bag? I braced myself all the more as the officer opened his mouth to speak. "I get off in 10 minutes. But I need to take a quick break. When I return from my break, I will need to write my report. Now, I am only going to write whatever I can see." *Why are you telling me this?* I thought. Then the Holy Spirit began to quicken me. I looked intently at the immigration officer to be sure of what he wasn't saying as he spoke again.

"If you need to use the bathroom, or the baby's diaper needs changing, you are going to want to use the one nearest the exit. Take the elevator down." He looked at Thomas and back at me again, "Now," he said with all seriousness.

I did not waste time. I darted for the elevator door. Akin quickly caught on and was at my tail. I moved with every ounce and energy I had until I made it to the elevator. I was one second too slow. Akin's brown, strong arm pushed through the elevator door right before it was about to close, his hand pushed it open and he moved into the elevator with me, staring down at me in discuss. "You're so stupid," he grimaced. "Where will you even go? You think any other man will want you?" I rejected his comment. "I'll go far away from you," I retorted.

"That's right. When they deport you!! I'm divorcing you. You will never make it here," then he laughed. "You'll never make it here. You can't make it anywhere." He leaned back against the elevator door, and it continued to slide down.

Something came over me. It was the same thing I would feel again a few years later- what I now know to be the anointing.

"Akin!" I called. He looked at me out of the side of his eye, disgust dripping from his flaring nostrils. "I will get my papers," I continued. "You won't just hear about it. You'll see it with your own eyes," I moved closer to him, unafraid. "And you're going to watch as I come and go, traveling as I please," I assured him as the elevator door inched open. We had reached the lobby.

Thank God, Papa was standing there at the exit. "Are you okay?" he asked, heading towards me as I inched my way out of the elevator with Thomas and his stroller. He looked Akin up and down as he awaited my reply. "Yes, Papa, please let's go, now!" Papa helped me with Thomas' diaper bag, and we moved quickly towards his double-parked car and packed ourselves inside, leaving Akin behind us.

It wasn't the last time I saw Akin. There were many more fights. But his father stayed by my side- even hired a lawyer. The lawyer he hired for my case was relentless. I got my papers. My parents back home were so thrilled to hear that I was safe and had finally made it legitimately in America. They paid Papa back every penny he spent on my lawyer. I thanked Papa for everything.

Getting my papers seemed a dream come true. Just as I'd forewarned, Akin watched in utter dismay and disbelief as I traveled to Nigeria and back and worked and went to school freely. He was in shock.

Getting my papers was not the end of all my troubles as I'd somehow deceived myself to believe. In fact, it was like the beginning of a new season of a series of heartbreaks and let downs. Akin disturbed my life until the day I was able to fully divorce him. After him came more and more pain until that day I found myself before my mirror, in tears.

Simi was the answer to the prayers I prayed that night I stood alone in my room in front of my mirror. He was the manifestation of a prophecy I didn't even realize I had and evidence that God always had something better planned for me. I always wondered if he knew how much he meant to me.

"Beloved," he called to me, gently, that day in the cafeteria, whisking me away from my trip down memory lane. "Things will get better, I promise," he smiled. I did, too. "I can promise that because God already promised us that," he confirmed.

In that moment, I thanked God with everything in me for Simi. I could not imagine continuing to live the life I was living before I met him- and before I truly met the God of my Salvation.

My mind went to Mercy, and I thanked God for her life, too. I still thought about what she said and how it hurt, but then I laughed.

'You don't know what it's like to be Dinah,' you say? My dear Mercy, I know Dinah's story better than you may ever understand.

I sighed a deep sigh of what I can best describe as divine satisfaction. God had finally graced me with enough peace to move forward. So, I stood up from the café table. "Alright, dear, let's go back and see our daughter," I announced to Simi. Simi smiled, as he always did, as he stood up from his chair, too. "Yes, our daughter, Mercy, that wants to be Dinah," he said. "Is she my daughter or Jacob's daughter? Or I don't know again," he went on sarcastically. "At least I know one way or the other, she's Abraham's seed," he laughed. Just then, a song came to my heart.

"The God of Abraham, Isaac and Jacob, Jehovah the Man of War….
His Mercy endureth forever… and ever…"

"And we'll bless His holy name!" we sang in unison as we made our way back to our beloved Mercy.

III.

YOU ARE DOING TOO MUCH

Unlike my mother, I spent most of my life fighting for life. I was born prematurely. Mommy jokes that the world was too excited for me to get here. I later determined that was a lie. I missed holiday after holiday fighting to breathe and to live, and not just because of my respiratory condition.

I am first generation Nigerian, born in America- and to two very Nigerian parents. As if the kids at school and their limited understanding of Africa was not enough, my mother who seemed to have left her home country without complaint loved to bring it here and force it down my throat and all over my life for the world to see. It was embarrassing. I could never fit in.

Many Nigerians have this thing about competition. They love to compare and decide who is best. If you are not the best, you might as well be nothing because you are only as good as who you are better than. I have two older brothers- both tall and handsome. Both very smart and outgoing. Both annoyed at how my respiratory problems seemed to slow them down in life. My mother was always proud of my brothers. She did not have to push them or motivate them. Excellence was in their blood.

"Mercy, there's a school play coming up- 'Matilda'. Did you see the announcement?"

"Yes, Mommy I saw. I'm not interested." I said firmly.

"What do you mean you're not interested? Why? The part is perfect for you." She insisted.

This is what she always did. Look for any opportunity to make some good out of me.

"Mommy, I have a lot of homework to catch up on. I missed a whole week of school, remember? I don't have time to study lines."

"Your brother used to memorize things all the time!" There she went again comparing me to my brothers.

"Mommy, then go tell Daniel to audition, please. I am not interested." Just then, my dad walked in the room.

"Honey!" Mom ran to his side. "Look at this!" Mom pushed my school newsletter in his face. Dad took the paper to see what all the fuss was about. "Tell Mercy this is a great opportunity for her. Look- there's a play at her school. Look at the main character. Isn't that so Mercy?"

"Oh, no, leave me out of this, please." Dad handed the newsletter back to Mom, grabbed what he wanted to grab and quickly exited, stage right. *Thanks for having my back, Dad.* I thought as I glared at him with contempt. I looked out the corner of my eye to see Mom was doing the same for her own reasons. I took a deep breath, "Mom, why are you always pushing me to do things I don't want to do?"

Mommy moved towards me, moving my bangs from in front of my eyes. "Because I believe you really do want to do it. You're just being stubborn. You're not shy. Sweetie, I am not trying to pressure you, I promise. But what kind of mother would I be if I did not push you to do what is best for you?" I rolled my eyes as she continued to talk. She smiled, with that reminiscent look in her eyes. "I remember when you were four years old. You still had your trach. You would watch TV shows and be jumping up and down acting like all the characters. You know every single line from that Frozen© movie. Those days, I was always yelling at your brother to keep quiet when he was watching and jumping up and down and he would pout, 'Mommy, you never yell at Mercy! She's being loud too!' And it was true! You were doing what he was doing and probably worse, but I didn't hear you. Look how far God has brought you! You have the opportunity to be loud and silly and have fun and everyone can hear you. I just want you to take advantage of it." I was not going to tell Mom she was right. What kind of twelve-year-old would I be if I just agreed with her and obeyed. "I am grateful, Mommy. I am. But right now, I'm just trying to keep up with my schoolwork. Please, just let me focus on catching up with my work so I can bring you good grades you can brag to everybody about." I was sure that would get her off my back. Mom shook her head and grinned, "Oh, alright, but don't say I didn't warn you. You're going to regret not auditioning.

Two months later, when I went to see our school play, I regretted not auditioning. I could have done way better than the little blonde-haired girl they'd chosen. Matilda didn't even have blonde hair in the movie. One of our Teenage teachers in church had mentioned taking on different activities and leadership opportunities as a means of increasing our influence and opportunities to share the Gospel. Maybe Mom was right that time, but she always came on so strong.

A few years later, I was in high school and had finally found myself, my personality, and my friend group and I was loving it. There were so many activities and opportunities to make friends and have fun in high school. Having spent much of my life in a hospital, I was excited to be in a whole new school, with people who didn't know me as 'Mercy, The Hospital Girl.'

I had changed. A lot. On the morning of my first day of high school, I took a long, hard, look in the mirror- something I seldom did while I was in elementary and middle school. I could hardly see the scar on my neck from the surgery I had where they were finally able to close it up. I had a set of chokers and selected a black and pink one that I felt matched my outfit of the day perfectly. I smiled.

Then, I put my hand on my belly. I only felt MY belly. No more G-tube. Just my God-given belly button. I recalled the days I chose to wear sweatshirts and oversized t-shirts to hide the bump I thought everyone could see under my shirt. Not anymore. I was so excited to wear my perfectly fitted shirt and jeans. Mom got on my nerves, but she was pretty cool when it came to shopping and helping me pick out the perfect outfit. Say what you want about the lady, she had style. Now, I felt I did too. Maybe even more style than Mommy.

I loved what I called my new body. I had gotten taller. I was about the same height as my mom. I loved how I looked in clothes. I loved myself and how much I'd grown.

I had braces now. Initially, I hated them. Daniel told me that everyone at school would call me 'metal mouth'. I told him to shut up. *God, please don't let people call me 'metal mouth'*, I prayed, just in case he was right. I was still recovering from being called, 'Mercy, The Hospital Girl' by a few of the devilish kids at my elementary school.

I don't know if this was God answering my prayer or not, but I learned there was a trending popstar- 'Koi Pond' known for her shiny, metallic braces and all the cool color rubber bands she would wear on them. My parents did not allow us to listen to secular music, so I didn't know much about her, but at school, people said I looked just like her. "Umm, no," I'd tell them, plainly. "I don't look like anyone less than God. I am the original, so if anything, Koi whatever her name is looks like me" Then I'd walk away leaving my peers dumbfounded, which apparently gave me a ton of cool points, boosting my popularity.

A few months into freshman year, the school posted auditions for the winter musical, Candy Land, starring a high school girl named Candy. The poster and the part of Candy brought to mind the experience I had a few years back when my mom's eagerness to intrude, and maybe some of my insecurities, kept me from auditioning. With my newfound popularity and church-nurtured vocals, I might be a shoe in for the role. Not to mention, everyone would find out I could sing- probably better than Koi Pond- and my high school popularity would be established forever. Sign me up! I auditioned, and call backs were just a few days later. I got the role and apparently, it was a big deal. Even the seniors were hyping me up about it, well the ones who weren't hating because I got the part over them.

One day, after our first rehearsal, some girls stopped me on my way out.

"Hey, Mercy. Great Practice," a girl greeted.

"Thanks, you were great too," I complimented.

"Where did you learn to sing like that? I took voice lessons at Madam Julliard's," the other girl shared proudly.

"I sing in the choir at church and with my family all the time," I responded, daring her to judge me for not going to some fancy singing school.

"Oh, that's cool. I wish my family had traditions like that. It sounds nice." I smiled at her interest in my life. The girl continued, "A few of us are going to Monty's after the game tonight. Want to join us?"

The two girls that stood before me were sophomores. What better way to solidify my social status than to be seen in public with almost upper-class men. I had to play it cool. I pulled out my cell.

"Umm, tonight? I think I could make that work. I airdropped her my contact details. "You'll text me the deets?"

"For sure," Girl one responded.

"Sweet. I gotta run. See y'all later," I smiled as I dashed off, pretending I had important things to do. I did actually. I had to get Mommy's buy-in.

I reached the house. Before I could greet, Mommy met me with her angry, Nigerian-mother face. "Kini eyi?" Mommy held her iPad in my face, "Kini eyi?" she asked again. "What, Mommy what is it? I can't see what you are talking about," I groaned. I was both nervous and annoyed. She shoved her iPad into my hands. I put my bookbag down and looked closely at an email from my school. It was the one they sent out monthly to all the high school parents. I read it and grinned small.

NORTHSIDE PREP CASTS FRESHMAN, MERCY ALABI, FOR LEAD IN WINTER MUSICAL. I skimmed through… ALABI IS THE FIRST FRESHMAN IN DISTRICT HISTORY TO BE CAST AS LEAD SINCE 1976. *Wow,* I thought to myself. *Not bad, freshman.*

"And you didn't even think to tell me so I can pray for you, or we can pray about it together. It says here the play is in one month. You have been going to rehearsals and doing things and you didn't tell me. I didn't even know! Kini gbogbo nonsense eyi? What kind of nonsense is this?" she went on.

"Mommy, it's not that big a deal, honestly. It's just a school play and I didn't tell you because I didn't want you making a big deal out of it," I reasoned. She looked at me speechless.

"Is it everything about my life I should tell you?" I shot back briefly, forgetting my mother was not like the other mothers in my neighborhood who gave their teens space and freedom. "That's not what I meant," I corrected before she ended my life. "I just mean I thought I shouldn't have to make an announcement every time I do something good because you raised me to do good in all that I do. Should I be making announcements every 5 minutes? No. I didn't mean to keep anything from you, honestly, Mom. I just wanted to do something good without all the pressure. I was going to tell you about the musical when the time was right. I wanted to surprise you and Daddy with tickets to the play a few weeks before opening night." I prayed in my heart my response would help me live to see another day. I exhaled as Mommy's face softened, though only slightly. "Mommy, I love you. I'm sorry. I didn't mean to offend you," I added as icing on the cake. I remembered I still needed to ask her if I could go out… on a school night.

"Hmm, so my daughter hasn't been in school 3 months, and she is breaking records," Mom grinned. "Mommy, stop it!" I laughed. "Wait until I tell your aunties. I heard your cousin tried out for basketball and they only placed him on junior varsity."

"Mommy, most freshmen start out on junior varsity," I informed her. "Not my daughter. She is starting her freshman year as the lead." My mom was grinning from ear to ear as she sauntered into the kitchen to prepare dinner and brag about me to my aunties.

"Mommy, guess what?""

"Yes, my baby," she was still smiling

"Some girls from the musical invited me out tonight for ice cream… to celebrate a great rehearsal," I grabbed a banana.

"Oh, tonight? A school night?"

"Yes," I took a bite, "But we won't be out too long. It's just walking distance down the street. Just to grab ice cream and talk small about the musical and planning, nothing big. We are meeting up at Monty's at six. I will be back by eight or eight thirty latest."

"But you know we have family prayer tonight by 7 pm. And what about your homework or practicing for this play of yours?" Of course, she would make this complicated.

"I'll do my homework and chores before I go, and can we please have family prayer when I get back?" I planned this all out in my head. No excuses, Mom.

"Who are these kids you're going out with?"

"Some kids from school, Mom.""'

"Kids from school don't have names?"

"Why does it matter, you don't know them."

"But do you know them?"

"I want to get to know them. That's why I really want to go. Don't you want me to have friends, Mom?"

"You have friends. You have your church friends. You're making friends at school. I just don't want you to lose focus."

"I'm focused. But I need to have fun, too. I'm finally able to have friends. This is the first time anyone has invited me anywhere that's not one of our church members. Mom, please can I go?" I begged.

Mom was quiet. I could tell she was trying to answer wisely. "Mercy, your life has to have structure. If you start interrupting your structure and changing your priorities every time for the sake of a good time, life will not go well for you. Plus, I want you to be safe. Not everyone who says they are your friend are your friends," she cautioned. Always overthinking things as usual. "You know what? If you do all you said, you can go…"

"Yes! Thank you, Mommy!"

"If Daniel goes with you."

"Oh, come on!"

"Mercy, you can't even tell me these kids' names. Daniel is cool and happening," she said trying to sound cool to no avail. "And he is close to your age. He can hang out with you, and it might even give you cool points." But I wanted to make my own way in high school, not live in my brother's shadow. "Mommy, please why can't you trust me?" I asked her. Truly, I wanted to know.

"Honey, It's not about trust. It's about what I know. Everyone who claims to be your friend is not your friend," she cautioned.

"But Mommy..."

"That's enough. That's your option, period." Mommy was done. There was no point in me trying any further.

"Yes, Ma" I responded in defeat as I left to quickly do my homework and chores.

My brother met me at the front of the house a few hours later. I walked by as if I didn't even see him, headed for Monty's Ice

Cream Parlor. "You're so rude," he commented. "You're so lame," I retorted. "I take time out of my day to walk you somewhere and this is how you treat me? Forget it, I'm going back home. I have other things to do," he turned around. I wanted to let him go but surely Mommy would see him and ask what happened and I would be forced to come home and might never have the opportunity to go with my friends on a school night again. "Okay, okay, I'm sorry. Just let's go, please." Daniel took pity on me and came back. We walked the rest of the way in silence.

We reached Monty's and my tummy did a somersault. There were girls from school laughing and joking together at a table…and a few boys to… upperclassmen. Some of them played football with Daniel. "Yo, Captain Danny Boy is in the house!"

"Hey Cap!"

"Captain, your mom let you out on a school night?" one of the guys yelled out. They all laughed. "We've never seen you off campus on a Wednesday night. Almost didn't recognize you!"

"Dude, shut up," Daniel grinned as he greeted his teammates with some over-the-top varsity handshake. "I'm actually just here spending some quality time with my sis. Ya'll know Mercy?" All the guys looked in my direction and smiled, some of them a bit devilishly and I wasn't sure what to make of it. Were they making fun of me?

"More like…Lord, have Mercy," I heard one of the boys mumble. "I think I need a little Mercy too," remarked another boy as his fist bumped the guy sitting next to him. One of the girls kicked him.

"What did you just say?" Daniel asked, ready to square up. "Actually, Mercy is here with us, right, girls? Come sit down, Mercy," one of the girls interrupted, the same one who told me about the get together. "Hey, everyone," I greeted, more shyly than I expected. I didn't count on any of the upper-class boys being there. "You guys ordered already?" I asked as I noticed everyone's milkshakes were more than half gone. "Oh yeah, we have been here for hours. I'm sorry we must have told you the wrong time. We were wondering where you were," she responded, looking at the other girls. "We are all heading to Mike's place now. You wanna roll?"

"Nah, we are good- we were looking forward to milkshakes. We will catch you later though," Daniel responded.

"We weren't asking you. We were asking Mercy," the girl glared at Daniel. "We are sorry, we didn't know she was bringing you so there's only enough space in my ride for her, unless you want one of us to sit on your lap, Quarterback," the girl said to Daniel somewhat flirtatiously. "I'm good. Come on, Mercy, let's order our shakes," he commanded. I didn't move. Did he think he was my dad? I could make my own choices. "Uh oh Cap! It looks like she wants to roll with us. Don't worry, Mercy. We have plenty of ice cream for you to lick at my place," a guy said as he stood up, walked towards me and put his arm over my shoulder, caressing my hair. I'd never received that kind of attention or affection from a boy before and shook a little, trying to be cool about it.

"If you don't take your hand off my sister, I'm licking the floor with your face," Daniel cautioned in the same calm tone my dad always used when he was not playing around. He even smiled like him. It was terrifying. Daniel boldly moved the guy's arm off my shoulder and waited patiently for him to retaliate. "Daniel, be cool," I whispered. The last thing I needed was for a fight to break out on my behalf, I'd never get to go anywhere again. "Please," I begged.

Daniel's eyes didn't blink or waiver as he backed up at my request, still smiling, like Daddy, but a bit scarier. "Let's go order our milkshakes, Mercy. We will catch you guys, later." He looked at the other girls, who looked terrified. "Stay safe, ladies!" he said to them with actual concern. "Tell your sister to stay safe. Don't worry, baby girl. When you're ready to grow up and stop hiding behind big brother, we still have that ice cream for you," the boy smirked.

Just then, as if by divine intervention, we heard the parlor door jingle and Thomas walked in. We hadn't seen in months. Mom told us he was coming to visit us from the Navy this weekend. I didn't expect him to show up today. No wonder Mom let me go for ice cream on a school night. "Thomas!" I exclaimed excitedly before I remembered I was supposed to be acting cool and that a war was about to break out in the ice cream parlor because of me. Thomas gave me a big hug. He had gotten so strong, and his perfume made him smell even more manly. I remembered when my big brother was so scrawny and always smelled like he had been rolling around outside.

Daniel was still boiling. Thomas looked over in Daniel's direction. "Danny boy, you're getting buff! You good? I thought you would be happier to see me," then he paused looking around. "…Is there a problem?" he asked, finally noticing the tension that was heating up the ice cream shoppe.

Thomas was still dressed in his dress blues. He walked over to Daniel and stood by his side as he stared at the boys trying to decide if they were ready to fight.

I am not sure if those boys were hesitant because Daniel was their beloved team captain or because they were seeing his African side. I am sure Thomas walking in dressed like Naval Commander didn't make their decision any easier, or maybe it did. "Is there a problem, Danny," my oldest brother repeated, firmly. He was talking to Danny, but his eyes were on the other boys. 'Sir, no Sir!" Daniel's eyes and rage still on the boy who dared put his hands on me.

Thomas nodded, "Good. Fellas, do we have a problem? Did my brother do something to you?" Thomas asked the boys. "Tell your brother…," one of the boys started, before his homeboy nudged him back to reality. "No, officer," he answered, alas. "No, officer. Thanks for serving our country. We were just leaving," the other kid responded as he signaled the rest of his peers to leave the parlor.

Daniel was still standing there livid. "Come on, boy, we getting milkshakes or what? Your big brother's back in town. Don't mind them. Drinks on me," Thomas laughed, pulling us both towards the counter. "Oh, and if I was you guys, whatever happened, I wouldn't tell Mommy. You know how she gets." Daniel took a deep breath and hugged our brother. I hugged him too as he ordered our milkshakes.

We went to sit down together to laugh and reminisce. As I drank my strawberry milkshake, I was grateful to be spending time with my brothers. I felt safe and kind of cool. But, still, I sat there wondering what I had missed out on. Then I remembered how angry I was that Daniel interjected. He was always interfering. I had always wondered what all the cool upperclassmen did, and thanks to him and Mommy being so overprotective, I would never know.

IV.

YOU CAN DO MUCH MORE

As Mercy grew older, all I could see was me. Dimple to temple, she was my split image. O jomi! She even carried my stubbornness and sense of adventure. The first time she asked me if she could meet up with her friends, I was tickled pink. It had always been so hard for her to make friends because she missed so many days of school and took so long to truly find her voice and identity. I never let Thomas or Daniel go out on school nights. They were very popular and used to beg and beg until they finally gave up and accepted that their time with God, family and focusing on their studies needed to be their priority. Both of them played sports and were heavily involved in school activities so they had plenty of time to connect with their peers in safe and structured, productive ways. My flesh wanted to tell Mercy, yes! Go enjoy your friends! Have fun and tell me all about it. My soul was afraid. What if it's a set up? What if they don't truly like her or something bad happens? But years ago, I made the decision and developed the habit of hearing the Spirit of the Lord when I needed to make critical decisions. The Holy Spirit was telling me to take caution. So, I did. I wanted to balance giving her the space she needed to develop her confidence and feel accepted, all the while keeping her safe. I knew she wouldn't be thrilled having her brothers with her, but I learned long ago to recognize and not be emotional about making critical decisions.

I could remember being her age and wanting desperately to fit in and to be accepted.

I was 14 when I arrived overseas with my aunt. The weather was so different- colder than I had ever experienced in my life. But my excitement warmed me. My aunt had three daughters, Demi, Bisi, and Lolade. I was so excited to finally meet them in person. They were all around my age and seemed so sophisticated on our phone calls and in the pics I'd seen.

We made it to my auntie's house just before sunset. Her house was beautiful, just as I expected. She lived in a quiet suburban neighborhood where all the houses looked very much alike. It was so different from the loud and busy city of Lagos I was used to. There were no giant gates around the homes as I was used to. You could see everyone's lawn and driveway. Some of them had cute and interesting decorations in the front.

She opened the door, and we were greeted well by her husband, my Uncle Lekan, and my three cousins. The house smelled delightfully of iyan and egusi and I was so grateful. It had been a very long plane ride with foods I did not understand, and I was starving.

My first few weeks in my auntie's house, I was very shy. I was still adapting to the culture, and every now and then, I couldn't help but feel my cousins were making fun of me. One day, they finally invited me to go out with them. I was so excited.

"Umm, is that what you are going to wear?" I didn't respond

right away. What was wrong with my outfit? "Come on, girl. Let us hook you up." They guided me into one of their bedrooms- Demi's. Demi's room was designed so elegantly, not drab and boring, the way my living area felt. Demi opened her closet. She had so many outfits and shoes. I'd never seen so many clothes in one space except at the market.

"Here. Try this," Demi smiled as she pulled one of them out of the closet for me. She had a lot of clothes, but her clothes didn't have a lot of fabric. I tried to play it cool and not seem too judgmental. "Wow, this is nice," I said, "But won't I be cold?" My cousins laughed. "Trust me," Bisi smirked, "The party we are going to will be full of options to warm you up." I was very confused. Would there be more clothes there? Lolade rolled her eyes as she pulled a small leather jacket from her sister's closet. "Here. You can wear this. You just can't go out with us looking like you just came from the village," All of them laughed. I was offended. My clothes were new and very nice. And not that there was anything wrong with growing up in any of the villages of my home country, but I was from the city. And as hot as Lagos city could be, we all still wore clothes that had much more material except we were ashewo (night workers).

I was still getting to know my cousins and didn't want to fight them yet. I just wanted to get out of the house and meet people. So, I didn't respond. I took the jacket. I wore the skimpy outfit. They helped me make up my face and I went with them to the party.

That night, I was exposed to a whole new world- a world I wasn't ready for. It started out fun. The music, the dancing. But then there were the drinks. I took my first one that night. One sip, then another. It made it easier to dance the way the guys wanted me to dance. I had been in the house, feeling so alone for months by this time. I learned years later that, all the while, I was supposed to be in school. My father was sending Auntie money every month. But instead of enrolling me, they told me I had to earn my keep. I spent most of my time doing chores around the house and watching them be a family. I was so happy to be out of the house and around people that I was ready to take any kind of attention. I received a lot of attention that night- attention I would later regret. "Don't be shy," a guy told me. I had never been so close to a boy in my life. "This is how we do things here in America," he said as he began to kiss me slowly in places I'd never been touched before. I left the party feeling dirty and low.

"Somebody had a good time at the party" Demi nudged as we left. "Yeah, I didn't think you had it in you. You always seem so uptight," said Lolade. "You had fun, right, Elizabeth?" asked Bisi.

"Oh… yes," I lied. The last thing I needed was for them to make me feel worse than I already did. We arrived home very late that night. Their mother was still at work and wouldn't be back 'til morning. I was sure we should be in trouble with their father. His car was in the driveway. I wondered if we would need to sneak in. But my cousins led me right through the front door. I braced myself for entry. I didn't see their father. I only heard music coming from upstairs.

"Come on, hurry up, let's go," one of them pushed me up the stairs. I moved as quickly as I could towards Bisi's room. All of us entered laughing and they quickly changed into night clothes. "Oh, my night clothes are in my room. I'll change there. Have a good night and thanks for inviting me out." My cousins laughed and rolled their eyes, continuing to laugh and joke as I exited, closing their door behind me. Uncle was still in his room. I quickly tiptoed to my own quarters to change. But I really had to pee. I grabbed my night clothes to quickly change in the bathroom after. I had been holding it the whole way home.

"So, they let you go with them," my uncle startled me as I came out of my room. "Sir..." I put my head down. I was busted. "It's okay, it's okay," he caressed my shoulder with his hand. "I'm glad you had some fun. Naughty girl!" I was so nervous. I didn't know what to think or do. I am sure I was shaking. Uncle bent to pick something up. When he did, I could feel is breath maul over my legs. "You dropped something." He handed me my underwear. I was so embarrassed. "Ehm, oh. So sorry, Sir," I stammered, eyes still to the ground. "It's okay. Wash very well." He instructed, as he moved out of the way to allow me to go into the bathroom. I bowed briefly and headed straight into the bathroom, closing the door, completely ashamed.

Did he know how we were partying? Did I smell like alcohol? Would he be waiting to sound me immediately I came out of the bathroom, or worse, would he tell Auntie? She would surely call my parents and I would be on a plane back to Nigeria in no time.

I took my time in the bathroom. When I came out, Uncle was

in his room. I thought I heard strange sounds coming from there, but Auntie wasn't due home for hours. I chose to ignore the groaning noises and head straight for my room. I had lots of chores to do tomorrow and wanted to get a good night's sleep. Or as much sleep as my conscience would allow.

A few weeks later, I was cleaning the bathroom when I heard a ton of commotion coming from the living room. "See my girls! Honor Students! See these grades! I am so proud of you all! Demi-you will go to Harvard, in Jesus' name!" Auntie was exclaiming.

"And Bisi, well done with your sports! I always enjoy watching your games, and you, too, Lolade with your dramas and your writing. You girls really make me proud," Uncle went on.

I hurried back into the bathroom and bawled my eyes out. I graduated from secondary school when I was 14, right before I came to America. But in America, they had what you call 'high school', where you studied until you were about 17. I wanted to go to high school or college or wherever I was supposed to go. I wanted someone to celebrate me.

Months later, all the celebration became much quieter when Bisi, my oldest cousin, put to birth. No one knew that all the while we were partying and she was going to school, she was pregnant. We had the baby quietly. She was beautiful with eyes like her mother. I think she looked a little like me too. Bisi still went away to school. I stayed home to take care of her baby up until the day I finally left.

I told myself, if I ever had a child, I would do much more for her. I would not leave her to be taken care of by mere strangers where she would be kept scrubbing toilets. I would make sure she could do fun things like play sports and do drama or whatever she wanted to do while she finished her studies. My child would be the best he or she could be. I was going to be sure of that.

V.

YOU DON'T KNOW ANYTHING

Thomas had been in the Navy for the past three years by now. I missed him dearly. We all did. I remember being so surprised when he told us he was leaving, then terrified when he informed us he would soon be deployed. *Why would you want to be so far away from us?* I recall thinking to myself. But, when I was older, I understood.

Thomas never said it, but I know he left to get a way… to be free and live his own life. I never really heard them talk too much about it, but I knew Mom never approved. She wanted him to go straight to college and live the life she designed for him. Now that I thought about it, she must have nagged Thomas just like she nagged me.

Being the child of Christian, African parents was

overwhelming. Everything always had to be in order- but the order was not your own. You were a slave to God, to your parents. Nothing you ever did seemed good enough for them. They cared less about your happiness and more about how your life reflected on them. Mom and Dad were always talking of destiny and calling. But what did they truly know about our destiny or what we were called to do.

God gave *us* these lives, not them. How could we be sure they were not just impressing their fears, insecurities and regrets on us? The world had changed so much since they were younger. Things weren't the same. Why couldn't they just get along with the times, instead of being so churchy and stuck in their old country?

I remember a time when Thomas wanted us to meet his new girlfriend, Monica, and Mom flatly refused. I never understood why. Why wouldn't you want to meet the person in your child's life? Was she afraid she was going to lose her influence over Thomas to his new love interest? I was very young at the time, so it wasn't my place to ask questions. I also didn't care too much back then as none of it really concerned me. But it mattered to me now. I was afraid that if I ever wanted to be free, I too would need to branch out on my own.

I was a straight A student. My grades were even better than my brother's grades ever were. I was involved in three clubs at school. I attended church three times a week and still, that didn't seem to be good enough. She wouldn't even let me date.

"Mom, I'm 17 years old, are you really serious?" I asked her after she flatly told me I couldn't go out on a date I had been asked on by my crush.

"Mercy, this is not up for discussion. You know our stance. We don't date in this house. We do courtship. Is this boy seeking your hand in marriage? If not, what are you dating for?" Mom was so unrealistic. No boy was thinking like that these days. "Mom, how will I know anything about being ready for marriage if you and Dad won't even let me have a boyfriend?" My mother looked at me with annoyance. "Really, Mercy? Have we not been teaching you about courtship and marriage since you were twelve years old in church? You can't look and learn from your father and I about healthy marriage? Try again."

Mom was impossible. I never imagined a guy would be into me. Brian Johnson was the cutest guy in my school. I secretly had a crush on him for the last two years, but I always acted like I was uninterested. Brian was smart. We were in honors bio together last year and AP chemistry together this year. He was secretly the reason I was doing well in science. I couldn't wait to make beautiful chemistry with him. He was charming. All the girls wanted him, and it was me that he was into. Mom wouldn't even let me go out on a date with him.

"Mommy, please. Can I at least invite him over for you and Daddy to meet?" I tried to reason, not that I wanted him to meet my embarrassingly overwhelming parents, but I was desperate.

"For what, Mercy? Can you tell me why he wants to meet us? Why he wants to date you? Have you finished your college applications? Your focus is everywhere but where it needs to be!" I remember she told Thomas something like that, too. Excuses. All these questions were just excuses to steal my happiness.

"I'm not going to college," I blurted. I watched my mother freeze in her tracks. "What did you just say to me?" She touched her ear signaling for me to dare to repeat myself. I dared. "I said I'm not going to college. I am going to live my life the way I choose. I am going on a date with Brian. In fact, I'm already his girl. I am doing a gap year. Maybe I'll join the Peace Corps or travel with a few of my friends. It's my life and I have to make the most out of it. Thomas did what he needed to do for his life. He chose the Navy, and he is happy! Heck, maybe I'll join the Navy too!"

Mother walked slowly towards me, staring me in the eye. Ordinarily, I knew to look down. But not today. I gave it right back to her. At this point, she was directly in my face. I towered over her. She didn't seem to notice that. "Thomas has his degree," she informed me, coldly. I was not sure a slap wouldn't follow. "And if you ask Thomas today, he wishes he had heeded my counsel. But to God be the glory, everything worked out for him. I think your dad and I's prayers had much to do with that. You have been healed and hospital- free for all of 5 years. Which army do you want to go to? Don't play with your life that I prayed for day in and day out for the past 17 years!"

That was a low blow. How dare she bring up my past medical condition? As she rightly stated, I was healed. How dare she insinuate that I'm somehow too weak to do well in the armed forces or in life without her and her arrogant prayers. As if my life depended on her prayers…. As if God would not have healed me on His own. God was the One who allowed her to give birth to me in that position in the first place.

I'll show her. I grabbed my car keys and dashed towards the front door. *Now, pray you can keep control over me.* I thought, viciously. "Where do you think you're going?" My mother demanded.

"Out with Brian, my boyfriend and to live my life."

"Ha! Out? To defy me… in the car I bought you? Lailai!" she snatched the keys from my hand. "Now, think well before you walk out of that door," she threatened. I was boiling. As if by divine intervention, my dad walked through the door. His presence wasn't enough to calm me down.

"I hate this house! I hate you!" I yelled in frustration. My dad was shocked. "Mercy, go to your room," he instructed quietly, without even knowing fully what was going on. I stared at him in disbelief. Was he not even going to ask my side of the story?

"Did I stutter?" he asked a bit louder. He wasn't even going to give me a chance to speak. *Unbelievable.* I thought to myself as I stormed up the stairs and to my room. I was crying on my bed when I suddenly felt a shift in the atmosphere. My mom had been yelling at my father about me, totally berating me for the past 5 minutes. Now, it was quiet. That usually meant my dad was talking. I sniffled a bit and went to my bedroom door to listen. My father was speaking in tongues. Then I heard my mother reluctantly join in. *Stupid religion*, I thought to myself. Then I felt a terrible smack to my cheek and feared God had heard my thoughts. It was only Daniel who burst into my bedroom without so much as a knock. "Oh, sorry," he apologized, "I didn't know you were standing there. Anyway, what the heck did you do?! Mom and Dad are down there speaking in tongues… the way they're going, neither of us will ever be able to go out. Again!"

I sat down on my bed. Daniel accompanied me. "Daniel, Mom is impossible. All I asked was to introduce her to Brian," I whined.

"Oh yeah, I heard you two are a thing. Be careful with him. I don't think he's really your type," Daniel commented.

"How on earth do you know what my type is?" I countered. Daniel was such a Mama's boy.

"I mean, he doesn't have the same values and stuff we have. His parents are never home, and he does whatever he wants, and treats girls however he wants. Just be careful, okay?"

"For your information, I know he didn't grow up in church,

but he said he wanted to learn. He even asked to visit our church. He thinks it's cool Mommy and Daddy are like celebrity pastors or whatever." It turned out dating was a great way to bring people to Christ.

"That sounds good. But he likes girls that are like a challenge for him. He will say anything to get what he wants. Anyways, I trust you- but whatever you said to Mom down there- you better fix it, or Brian will definitely be meeting Jesus much sooner than planned with the kind of prayers they're down there praying. Are you grounded or what's going on?"

"I don't even know…" I responded before Dad's voice interrupted.

"Mercy!" He bellowed.

"Well, we are about to find out. The Lord have mercy on Mercy, in Jesus' name. No pun intended," he snickered quietly so my parents wouldn't hear. He was a jokester, even in times like this.

I walked slowly down the stairs. Did I even want to hear what they had to say?

"Sit down," Daddy ordered. I sat down on the couch. Mom was silent and did not look my way. "Now, in this house we have rules. And we did not come up with these rules arbitrarily. They exist to keep you safe and to preserve your destiny. We want you to live the best life God has made available to you." I continued to sit and listened to Daddy's speech- one that wasn't new to me. It's only that his tone was different this time. "What you said to your mother or into the atmosphere or whoever you were yelling at when I arrived was foolish beyond words." I guess he wanted an apology. "Fine, I am sorry. May I please be excused? I have chores I didn't finish. I accept whatever consequence you want to give me," I said, hoping to speed the process up.

"Well, I'm glad to hear you say that." Daddy grinned. I rolled my eyes. "Since you hate us and you hate this house God has blessed us with, I am thinking maybe you don't want to be here. The food, and lifestyle we give you seems to be causing you much pain based on how you were yelling. You are not 18, so by law, you have to live here, and we have to give you a roof. Maybe you want to stay in the garage? Would that be better for you or where did you have in mind to live if not in this house that you hate?" he asked. I know he expected me to beg for forgiveness and yield to their ridiculous rules, but my pride would not let me. I was tired.

"Honestly, I don't care," I responded nonchalantly. His scare tactics were not going to bother me today. "I'll go to the garage. It's fine. I just can't have this talk anymore, please, Sir."

"Ha, this girl," he laughed and looked up to the heavens, then at my mother who still refused to make eye contact with anyone.

"Well," he replied, "If you go there, it won't be for free. That is still my property and part of this house that you hate. You have no job to pay rent, so why don't you clean it and earn your keep, my prodigal daughter?"

"Whatever, no problem. Thank you, Sir," I responded sarcastically.

"And please," he continued. *There's more?* I thought to myself. "Thank you for returning our car key. We will take the phone that we paid for and the iPad that we bought you also. I'm sure you hate them, too," he said, as I headed to the garage. "You can take it. It's in the room you just put me out of. Thank you so much, Sir," I responded as I went to angrily clean the garage in response to Daddy's petty request.

The garage was a dusty mess. I didn't mind cleaning it as much as my father seemed to think I would. Our garage was heated and well lit. It had more spiders than I cared to be near, though. But there was an old futon, a minifridge and a tv, in case Daddy seriously made me sleep out there. Cleaning helped me to calm down anyway, so I didn't mind the distraction.

Being out there, in the garage and out of earshot made it that much easier to tip out and see Brian. I just needed to figure out a way to text him. There were lots of old tech in the garage I could easily rig up enough to Snapchat him. I'd figure something out as I cleaned up.

About two hours had gone by. I'd taken a brief nap but had still gotten plenty done. I had found an old iPhone and was able to access my Snapchat to see messages from Brian. He wanted to see me right then. I told him I'd meet him at Monty's around 10 pm. My parents would be asleep or on a prayer line somewhere. They would be occupied long enough for me to spend, at least, two hours with my love. I told him we could hang out 'til Monty's closed… or maybe 'til the sun came up- I'd just need to be home before 5 am to settle in. Brian agreed and said he couldn't wait to see me.

The excitement of seeing Brian and the brief nap I'd taken had me full of energy. I was overcome with excitement, adrenaline rushing all through my body as I daydreamed of the love adventure that awaited me. I decided to put that energy to use organizing our family photos and important documents.

I was organizing a box of old dusty pictures when I found an old ultrasound pic. It was of Daniel. I'd seen it before, so I put it back down. But it struck me. I'd never seen mine… or Thomas'. I wondered why. I decided to go through the box carefully. Daniel was the middle child. Most parents had everything for their first child and then got lazy later… or they had easily accessible pictures of their youngest baby, but not the oldest ones. Maybe Daniel really was the family favorite. I kept digging. Alas, I found something. Our birth certificates. There were two things that took me completely off track. In my hand, I held four birth certificates. The first one that caught me off guard was Thomas'. Who was Akin Adeoye? Why was his name there in the place of my father's? And my mother had three children. Why was I holding four birth certificates? Who was Michael? Why did he have my birthday? This was all too much. I had to get out the house.

I grabbed the old iPhone I'd found.

WYD right now, I snapped to Brian along with a pic of myself in distress.

Waiting for you, he snapped back, looking more handsome than ever.

I fixed myself up in the broken mirror near the back door of my garage. No purse, no make-up. I didn't care. I quietly tipped out the garage backdoor, bringing with me an old bag with a folder of everything I found- all the lies and secrets my mother had been holding since before I was born.

"I thought you wouldn't make it tonight… and here you are earlier than I even expected. I was surprised when you hit me up," Brian smiled as I squeezed in next to him on the bench. "Yeah, well today has been one for the books." We hugged. He smelled of some kind of fancy cologne.

"I'm so glad to be out of the house," I commented as Brian signaled the waitress over to take my order. I remembered I didn't have my purse. "Oh, I'm okay. I left my wallet," I informed him.

"Are you kidding? You're my girl," he said. "Excuse me, miss, she will have the mint milkshake." *How on earth did he know the exact milkshake I wanted?*

"Trouble with the parents again?" he asked as he took a sip of his own.

"Yeah, something like that," I responded elusively.

"Let me guess. Your mom, right? Is she tripping again?"

"Tripping is an understatement…"

"That crazy lady has my girl tripping, what did her holiness do this time?" he smirked as he caressed my cheek. I gave him a half smile, looking down at the old bag on my lap containing the folder as I tried to decide if I should tell him about everything I found in the garage- my brother's mystery father…the ultrasounds…my secret twin brother's birth certificate… the fact that my mother was a liar.

"I don't really want to get into it." I chose instead. He seemed surprised that I didn't want to share.

"Really? Okay well… how about we go to my place… and get into something else?" I shivered. I'd never been to his place before…. or any guy's place, for that matter. But Brian was special. There was something about him. He gave me so much attention and didn't expect me to perform all the time. I could be weak and shy around him, but I could also be passionate and energetic.

He seemed to love everything about me. He always complimented me on my looks, my singing and my drama performances. He loved that I was smart. In fact, I was the only girl he trusted to help him do his homework and study for his tests in our AP science classes. He told me that without me, he would have been kicked off the football team or reduced to taking basic science classes. Brian was popular and girls were always vying for his attention, but I'm the only one he gave it to.

"What's at your house?" I asked him, coyly.

"Hmm, good question," he smiled.

"What's at my place? Well, I have a pool table. And a pool. No parents." He grinned.

"Well, I can't swim or play pool and I've never been without adult supervision before. So, I don't know if any of those incentives are worth my while." I smiled as I received my mint milkshake. I took a sip. "How about you get a break from that mother of yours?" he suggested. "Or I can just take you home, if that's what you want," he shrugged.

"I definitely don't want to go home." I grinned. He grinned and that's when I got my first real kiss. I was over the moon. Tonight would be a night to remember.

"Mercy!"

My eyes had been closed as my lips were pressed against Brian's, but they opened in terror when I heard the deep, dominant voice of my father.

"Get in the car. Now!" he commanded. I got up without uttering a word. I was almost too ashamed to be embarrassed. Brian was frozen in motion. He looked like he wanted to greet my father, but fear advised him against it. Old bag clutched in my hand; I went quietly to the car. Daddy looked violently at Brian and then looked away as he followed me to the car. Neither of us said anything until we reached the house. But before I went in, I remembered what I held in my hand. My fear and shame quickly turned to indignance and anger.

"I have a meeting now. But I will tend to you when I am done. I trust I don't need to tell you to be in this house when I am ready to talk to you." I didn't respond. My mind was on what I was ready to tell my mother.

VI.

YOU THINK YOU KNOW EVERYTHING

"You're a hypocrite!" There stood my seventeen-year-old daughter. Her face and eyes ice cold, as they stared into my soul. She was shaking. Though her stare was cold as ice, she was heated. I was sitting on my bed, with my Bible, Concordance and notebook, studying in preparation for a Bible study lesson I planned to take the next day. God had given me peace that Mercy was okay, so I decided to take my mind off the stress she was causing me to spend time in His word. Had I heard her well? "Excuse me," I asked, to be sure I heard right. "And where the hell have you been, young lady, how dare you leave this house…?"

"You're a hypocrite," she interrupted. "A liar and a hypocrite!" She yelled, tears in her eyes. "Me and Daddy have the perfect marriage. No boyfriends. No sex before marriage," she mocked. It was only then I noticed the documents shaking in her sweaty, angry hands.

She stormed into my room, livid, and dashed the birth certificates of my children over my study materials. I quickly picked up Michael's. "How did you..." I started but could not get my question out.

"What the hell is going on?" she demanded. "Is Thomas not my brother? Is Daddy even our father?" she screamed hysterically, tears rolling down her face. Just then, Daniel and Simi entered. Neither of them said anything right away. Simi was appalled. I was still sitting on my bed. A tear rolled down my cheek.

"Tell me the truth! Who is Michael?" Simi looked like he had seen a spirit and struggled a bit to catch his breath and find balance. Daniel was confused but tried to remain calm and help his father sit down.

But then he spoke, "I used to have dreams about that name. Michael. I just remember one day you were crying so badly, Mom. It was when you brought Mercy home. I remember Big Auntie and Uncle came and talked to you in the other room while I was playing my games." Daniel looked reflective. He continued to talk. "Dad looked so sad, I remembered thinking. I was afraid to ask him what was wrong. He had been down from the moment he came home that morning. I think he either came from the store or the hospital seeing you, Mercy." I watched him look at his sister as he went on. "Then, after Big Auntie and Uncle came, I can't forget the screaming. I dreamed about it for weeks, and every so often I still dream about it. Michael! Michael! And I always wake up afraid. Mommy, who is Michael?" he finally asked me.

I felt weak. But I recounted how God brought me through and how he'd healed Mercy completely. I was so deeply depressed, and he healed me, and it wasn't the first time. I looked down at my bed preparing to talk when I realized it wasn't only birth certificates Mercy had thrown on my bed. There were ultrasounds. Ultrasounds of every baby I ever lost. I broke down and cried. I picked up each one and held it close to my heart. Then I took a breath and responded. Simi placed his caring hand on my thigh in comfort, knowing this conversation would not be an easy one. "It's easy in Jesus' name. You are strong, Beloved." He'd read my mind. I was ready to talk.

"Mercy, Michael is your twin brother. You were both born prematurely. But Michael didn't make it." I heard Simi sobbing beside me. Mercy stood silently. "Well why didn't you tell me? Why didn't you tell us? Does Thomas know?" she demanded.

"Yes, Thomas knows. He was older. We thought we might talk with you two about it someday, we just never knew.... You were really sick in those days, and we never wanted what happened with Michael to reduce your faith...Also, somehow, we just thought you knew. I am sorry we did not talk to you guys about this more. It was so hard losing our baby boy..."

"What about Thomas' birth certificate," Mercy interrupted, as if she completely dismissed everything that we had just shared with her. "...and the other babies in the ultrasounds?" she questioned.

"I was married before. That man's name you see there is Thomas' birth father, and yes, Thomas knows. He accepted your dad as his own because your dad has consistently been a father to him since we married. These babies are all babies I lost over the years. Babies that were too good for this world that God chose to take home. Do you have any more questions, Mercy, or are you done deflecting and looking for reasons to be angry because you don't like the rules that we have set for you in this house?"

"You see? That's exactly what I'm talking about! You are so

selfish! You have an excuse for everything. Everything is about you and has to be your way, but you never followed your own rules," she huffed. "You are giving me rules you obviously didn't follow. What with all your baby daddies and all," she snuffed.

"Enough!" It was the first time any of us had heard Simi raise his voice for anything besides high praises and his precious Eagles when they scored the winning goal. We all froze in shock. He stood up from the bed and walked towards Mercy. "How dare you talk to your mother like that and in my presence!" Mercy said nothing- her face still seething.

"You think you know better," Simi continued. "You think you know everything. You have the audacity to let me find you after you snuck out of this house in the night like a street walker. And you accuse your mother. The one who gave birth to you. The one who labored for you. The one crying tears because of you right now. You don't know anything. You are ungrateful! Unthankful! Inconsiderate of what your mother and I, and even your brothers, have sacrificed for you. This is how you thank us? With your immature and ignorant sense of judgment and desire to make foolish decisions? Walking in disobedience… If not for God, I…"

"If not for God what, Daddy?" she dared interrupt her father. "If not for God, Thomas wouldn't be a bastard with a father we never met? Or if not for God, Mommy would not have all these unborn babies that never saw the light of day? If not for God, my parents would not be religious lunatics? Without Him, my twin brother would not be de-?" Simi's hand swept across her face before she could finish her sentence. "Simi! Calm down!" I pleaded. But it was too late. "You see! I knew you hated me. I agree with you. Michael should be here, right? Not me, your bad, sick and unholy daughter that keeps you in prayer. I don't blame any of your children for leaving you. Well, me, too, I wish I died instead of him. In fact, don't worry, I will join them." With that, Mercy stormed out of the house.

VII.

YOU'VE GONE TOO FAR

Outside was cold. I did not care. A part of me wanted to look back and see if any of them had followed me. But a stronger part of me said that I should run and never look back.

About a year ago this time, I'd asked if I could live with my Auntie Kemi. Auntie Kemi was cool. She was my dad's sister and she understood what it meant to grow up in the States. She was a single mom with two daughters. She was strong. She was fun and carefree. She didn't take life as religiously as my parents. Her kids enjoyed freedom. True freedom. In my home, we didn't have a curfew because we did not need one. We could not go out on school nights unless it was a school- or church-related event. Weekends weren't much different. Auntie's kids got to hang out until 10 pm on school nights and 11 pm on weekends.

We visited Auntie Kemi sometimes for holidays. "You should sleep over some time," she suggested to me once before. "I know my brother can be intense. I can't imagine him being my father!" We both laughed. "We would have so much fun- you, your cousins and I," she urged. She knew I was the only girl among my siblings and understood how hard it was having all older brothers and parents like mine. I asked my mom if I could spend weekends with Auntie Kemi and she had said no without even considering my feelings. I told Auntie that my mom said I could not spend the night and that I wished I could live with her instead of my rigid parents. Auntie was so chill and so compassionate. "Oh, so sorry, baby. But you are welcome over anytime," she asserted.

I wondered if that offer was still good. I was too embarrassed to reach out to Brian, my boyfriend. I realized I didn't really trust any of my close friends at school to tell them what I was going through without it becoming the talk of the town. By now, I'm sure the whole school knew how crazy my dad was. No need adding more chaos to the story. Brian was probably too embarrassed to ever be seen with someone who had parents like mine again.

I thought about reaching out to someone from church,

maybe one of my church friends or one of the youth ministers. But my pride would not allow me. I knew what they would say and that it would not be what I wanted to hear. I sighed and shivered as I continued to walk aimlessly. No phone. No car. I did not want to go anywhere I knew my parents would look for me. If they searched for me at all. *God, what do I do? Where can I go?* I prayed silently.

"Mercy, is that you?" I heard a familiar voice calling me from across the street. The person walked towards me. I knew her. She was a girl from school. She wasn't part of the in crowd per se. But there was something cool about her. Everyone seemed to like or at least respect her.

"Hey, Anjoli," I tried to sound cheerful and cool. "What are you doing out this way… and so late?" I thought maybe she had a date or something. I'd never known her to date. Also, she was wearing sweats. Sweats could mean she was sneaking out. It would be interesting finding out the juicy details of her secret love interest. As long as it wasn't my Brian.

"Oh, don't tell anyone, but I teach a self-defense class up the street. I had to clean and lock up today. I was about to catch an Uber home… unless you drove- I would happily take a ride!"

"No!" I was almost busted and had to play it cool. "I'm not with my car today," I responded nonchalantly. She looked at me quizzically as if she knew I was holding back. I gave in.

"I got into it with my parents," I confessed. "Just taking a walk and getting some air, you know… trying to figure things out." I was too ashamed to admit that I was cold and afraid.

"I see. I wish my parents were around for me to get into it with," she replied. That's when I realized I'd never seen or even heard of Anjoli's parents. She never talked about them. Most of the kids at my school always had a reason to either brag or complain about their parents. I didn't recall Anjoli ever having anything to say about hers. "Where are your parents? Working?" It was late. I assumed her parents wouldn't let her travel alone this late unless they had no choice.

Anjoli paused, carefully considering her words or if she wanted to tell me the truth, I suppose. "My mom was deported last year," she finally said. I never realized she was from an immigrant family, too. "I eventually went to live with my aunt while my dad was figuring things out and trying to help my mom, but things were not going too well living with her and my dad ended up having to leave the country too. Long story short, both my parents are in Haiti. And I am emancipated."

"Emancipated? Meaning…" I tried to follow.

She smiled as she began to break it down for me. "Emancipated meaning I am my own guardian. I live independently as an adult. I just have to stay in school and keep a job. So far so good," she smiled.

"Anjoli, I did not realize that you went through all that. I'm sorry about your parents. Wait… you mean to tell me you have had your own crib this whole time… and you've never thrown a party?" I'm sure that wasn't the most appropriate way to lighten the mood, but I didn't know what else to say. She laughed. "I have been known to throw a few small kickbacks in my day. But no, I don't have time to party. I have bills and homework and ministry stuff."

"Ministry stuff?" I asked.

"Yeah, I'm a Christian. It's an important part of my faith that I stay active and serve, and you know, do Godly assignments and stuff, so I stay on track in life and destiny." She sounded like she had been raised by my mother with all that talk about destiny.

"Hmm. I am a Christian, too. I just don't think it's all that serious. We are young. We are already saved. We can just live our lives, you know. We're still human after all," I said, somewhat defensively.

"I hear you. Well, my destiny is very serious to me. I don't think I could make it without losing my mind if I didn't have Jesus and a purpose or whatever. Living out my faith is what keeps me grounded and focused. Otherwise, I think I would be lonely and bitter," she responded. I secretly envied how she was taking everything I'd learned about growing up so seriously. It all seemed ridiculous and dramatic to me over the years but Anjoli's explanation kind of made sense.

"It must be nice having so much freedom," I tried to change the subject. "You know, being emancipated and all. Too bad things didn't work out with your aunt, though," I commented. I was hoping she would tell me how cool it was being so free.

"Yeah, and I always liked my auntie when I was younger. My parents just knew I was in good hands with her. But when I moved in with her in middle school, things just got really weird, really quick. Protective services were involved. It was a lot. Life with her was so different. She had her family. I realized that I was kind of like second class in her eyes. I missed my parents. I felt so alone. I eventually found out that once I turned 16, it was an option for me. A case manager helped me through the process. She thought it would be good for me since I was doing good in school and had my church family and stuff. So, I did everything to make it happen. Figured if I was going to feel alone, I might as well live alone. But with God, I'm never alone."

"Whoa. So, you really live by yourself?" I asked, still kind of in disbelief. "Yeah," she laughed. "Do you want to come over?"

"Sure, if it's okay," I agreed, appreciative for a way out of the cold.

"Of course, it's okay. I make the rules in my house, and you are more than welcome." We both laughed as she called us an Uber. "I always thought you were super mature," I told her. "Now it all makes sense."

Anjoli lived in a small studio apartment. Before I noted the size of her home, I noticed how peaceful it was. I felt at rest immediately I walked in. She directed me to a small breakfast table that seated three. It had the cutest and most comfortable dining chairs. I sat and relaxed. For the first time that night, I was able to exhale. I saw on her coffee table, a Bible, notebook and writing utensils. She was really serious about all the ministry stuff. I thought about where my Bible was. It was either in my nightstand or in my "Church bag" where it would stay until Sunday. I was almost deep into my existential crisis when I realized I had bigger things to worry about. Anjoli lived in a studio apartment. It looked like her bed was also her couch. Unless I wanted to sleep on her floor or in her bathtub, I needed to figure something out.

"Anjoli, can I use your phone?" I asked. The only numbers I knew by heart were my own. And my mom and dad's cell numbers. I definitely was not calling either of them. I had a better idea. I signed into my IG account and used the chat feature to contact my aunt. Auntie Kemi always said I could come over any time. It was time to see if she was telling the truth.

"What's your address, Anjoli?" I asked her. She told me and I messaged it to my aunt. Me and Anjoli chatted for a while. "Oh, looks like you have a message," Anjoli informed me. I prayed it would be good news. It was. "My aunt is on her way. Thank you so much,"

"My pleasure. Thank you for keeping me company," she replied. Anjoli offered me some snacks while I waited, and it dawned on me that I had not taken any food besides a sip of milkshake since morning. I had this habit of always saying, "No, thank you" when people offered me snacks in their home. Anjoli went on, "I know it's not as fancy as what you eat at home, but it won't kill you. This meat pie is a snack we eat back in my home country, I buy it like every other week from the Haitian bakery a few blocks over. It's one of my guilty pleasures. This looks like beer. It's not. I'm a Christian, remember? It's malt. It's sweet. Try it." I laughed and Anjoli almost took offense.

"I'm not laughing at your food. I'm laughing because it's my food. My parents are Nigerian, and we eat meat pie, and we drink malt. Our meat pie just probably tastes much sweeter than Haitian meat pie." We both laughed. "Ha, I didn't realize you're from the Motherland. I have many Nigerian friends at my church. I almost would not have believed you, but the fact that you just sat here to defend Nigerian meat pie is the most Nigerian thing…" We laughed even harder, together. "Let me warm this up for you, then. "Thank you," I told her. When the food came out of the microwave, I ravished it. I ate two meat pies. I drank the whole malt and a bottle of water in what had to be less than ten or fifteen minutes. "Are you sure Haitian meat pie is not better? The way you tore that food up tells me Naija can learn a thing or two from the island about meat pie…I'm just saying…"

"Whatever, I can't lie, this was good though. Thank you so much."

"Oh girl, no problem at all. I'm just happy to have some good company today." Anjoli paused. It seemed like she wanted to ask me something. I used a napkin to wipe my mouth. "What?" I smiled. "Nothing," she responded. "Well, yes. I do want to ask you something."

"Okay, what's up?" I responded.

"Can I pray with you?" No peer outside my small group at church had ever asked to pray with me before. I was very caught off guard. Did she see me as a total sinner?

"Obviously you and I have different situations, but I know what it's like having to make difficult decisions. I remember being so mad at my mom when she got deported. I was mad she was so careless. I was humiliated because- I never even realized she wasn't a citizen. I was mad we were immigrants. I got made fun of so much growing up for the things my mom used to pack for lunch, for being poor and for the clothes I wore. Then I was mad at my dad because I felt he chose my mom over me. I was angry at God, too, for … everything." I listened carefully as Anjoli shared her story.

"We were in church like every other day. And it felt like nobody at church could help me. God couldn't help me. But it was a member at church that learned what was happening to me at my auntie's house wasn't good. She helped me to get help and even let me stay with her and worked with child services to keep me from going into like full out foster care with a bunch of people I didn't know. My church family prayed with me and helped lead me to Christ and forgiveness. They even helped me get this place. I talk to my parents every day and I'm even able to send money home to them to help the rest of my family. I am going to file for my parents next year when I turn 18. It might be hard with my mom's situation, but nothing is impossible with God. Anyway, I don't know your whole situation. I just know what I know you know. Nothing is impossible with God. And no matter what our situation or whatever we are going through, we don't have to go through it by ourselves."

I was almost moved to tears. "Yeah, we can pray," I bowed my head. "Heavenly Father, Eternal Rock of Ages," Anjoli went on. She used scriptures I had known all my life, but they hit differently on this night as she used them to practically save my life. "In Jesus' mighty name we have prayed…"

"Amen," we said in unison. I heard a horn beep. Anjoli looked outside her apartment window. "Is this your auntie?" I went to look as well. "Yep, that's her," I responded, as I went to gather my belongings only to remember that I came with nothing. I thanked Anjoli once more and gave her a hug. "Hey, take some of the best meat pie ever for the road," she snickered as she handed me a plastic bag with a container of meat pie, two malts and a bottle of water. "Naija no dey carry last. Especially not when it comes to meat pie," I smiled. "One day I'll come and make some for you and you will know."

"I look forward to it," she replied. I waved goodbye to Anjoli and thanked her once more as I went down the stairs, out the door and finally got into the car with Auntie.

"Care for meat pie?" I asked as a clever way of greeting. She stared at me, awaiting a proper greeting and explanation. "Good evening, Auntie. Thank you for coming to pick me," I looked down at my lap waiting for to say something. Anything.

"No. I don't care for meat pie; I care for an explanation. It's the middle of the night. What on earth is going on?" she asked, very concerned.

"It's a long story…"

"Well, good thing we have a long ride. Start from the beginning," With that, she put the car in gear and drove off, ears wide open.

After I had given her all the details, she was quiet for a moment.

"Mercy!"

"Yes, Auntie?"

"You mean, your parents don't know where you are 'til now?"

"No, Auntie, they don't."

"Hey, ya. You have to call them," she instructed.

"Auntie, please. I really don't want to go back home right now."

"Ah, I'm not saying you have to go home. I am saying you can't keep them worrying. It's not right. You can stay with me as long as you like or as long as they allow, but you have to let them know. Take my phone." I obeyed, but dreaded it.

The phone rang and I held my breath. I could feel Auntie pulling over. She knew this would be an intense moment. I hated that she pulled over where she did. We were not close enough to her house. That meant she might still decide to turn around and take me back home once she heard my mother's threats. I took one more look at Auntie. She was still staring and awaiting my follow through. She wasn't backing down. I sighed. "Auntie, your code." She used the facial recognition to unlock her phone. "Now hurry up. It's late," she said firmly. I was all out of time and excuses. I dialed. A familiar, anxious voice answered. "Auntie Kemi..."

VIII.

YOU'RE GETTING TOO CLOSE

"Hello, Mommy, it's me, Mercy," she answered quietly. "Honey, she picked… she picked! It's her!!" I snapped my fingers hastily, signaling Simi to hurry over. He ran over, eyes wide, "Is that Mercy?" I nodded frantically. "Yes!" I inched closer to him so he could hear our daughter's voice with me.

"Mercy…" I quivered. I thanked God Almighty for the opportunity to hear my baby's voice. Every story I ever heard about people's children who ran away and were never seen again raced through my mind. Many of my own experiences that happened when I was away from home flashed before me. God calmed my heart until I felt undeniable peace. I breathed.

"Mercy, where are you?" I asked, as calmly as God helped me to be. When she didn't answer, my flesh took over immediately.

"Where are you?!" I demanded loud enough for every devil to hear.

There was a long pause. All I heard was her breathing. Finally, she responded, "I'm heading to Auntie's house, Mommy." She waited for me to respond. I did not. “She said I could stay with her. I told you before, I wanted to stay with her,” Still, I said nothing. “Mommy, I’m staying with Auntie. I'm not coming back. I don’t want to! I can’t!" She hurled those words like a dagger, straight through my heart.

“Easy! Easy!” I heard Kemi whispering to her sharply in the background. My heart, bloodied from the violent burst of insults from my own daughter, dropped. I would have dropped the phone... but Simi stepped in as he always did and kept it from falling.

“Mercy, you left this house without telling us. You’ve never done anything like this before. Surely the devil is at work. I won’t have him win. You can’t allow him to win either.” Simi took a pause. Then he continued. “It’s good that you called your auntie. At least we know that you are okay,” Simi then looked over at me. Right then, I knew he was about to say something I would not like. I made sure he could see the fragility in my eyes. I couldn’t stand any more negative news in my life. Not tonight. For a few hours, I thought I had lost my daughter to the streets or to God knows where.

"It's late," he said finally to Mercy… and to me. "You can stay with your auntie tonight," he finalized.

"What?!" I screeched in disbelief. "No," I was putting my foot down. He wasn't thinking. He was responding to the moment and not looking at the big picture. "She needs to come home. Now!" I commanded. Simi said nothing back. As if he knew his word was final. "Unbelievable!" I howled.

"Give me the phone," I heard Kemi say to Mercy. "Mommy Mercy, this is Kemi your big sister. Listen. Your oga is right. It's late. Very late. It has been a long night for everyone. What we need is rest and we can sort things out in the morning. The most important thing is she is okay. She had wisdom to at least call me. You raised her well! We will deal with her for sneaking out. But for now, let us all rest. Please. Lest our anger get the most of us."

I hated that Kemi was right. So, I said nothing. Simi could deal with it from there. "I'm going to pray." I left Simi with the phone and went to my secret place. On the way to my secret place- a little room in my basement where I go to pray- I stopped at the kitchen for a cup of water. I sat at my kitchen island and the tears began to flow out. Thoughts of my past and things that had happened to me weighed heavily on my mind, but instead of my face, in those moments, I saw Mercy's and I cried even harder. I couldn't hold back the tears or the thoughts or the pain any longer.

"Where did I go wrong?" I thought aloud. I did not realize I had spoken aloud until I heard a familiar voice.

"You did not do anything wrong, Mom." It was Thomas. I quickly sniffled and tried to tuck away my tears. But I could not. Thomas held me tightly in his arms. I remembered when I used to do the same for him when he was a little boy. He was not little anymore. In this moment, he was strong and safe.

"Mommy, remember when I didn't want to go to college?"

"You wanted to run off with that stupid little girl," I sniffled. "The one that eventually broke your heart. How can I forget?" We both chuckled. Thomas sat down next to me. "Well, the only way I knew to break things off with her was because of what you taught me over the years," he responded.

"Hmm" I finally took a sip of my water.

"Mommy, I used to think you were so overbearing."

I looked at him and he was shaking his head as if the weight of those memories of me were too heavy to bear. Was I really that bad of a mom? "I'm sorry, Thomas…" He cut me off. "No, Mom. I mean… you are A LOT!" We both grinned. "But I have been around longer. So, I have seen some of the things you have been through that the others don't know about." He sat down next to me at the counter. "That's why I can understand Mercy's frustrations. She doesn't know everything that goes on in your head. Just like I did not understand before. You forget the number of times I called myself running away. At least, she didn't run all the way to the armed forces… she didn't, right?" I realized I had not even given him an update. "Well, there is a time she threatened to run and join the military like you!"

"Oh, really?!" we laughed.

"I will tell you that story another time," I told him. I noticed his phone blinking. I was sure it was his wife.

Thomas was supposed to be spending time with his family. He was newly married and his wife, who I'd recently grown to take a liking to, Regina, had given birth to the most beautiful baby girl just a few weeks ago. They named her Isabel. She had my eyes. They had a place a few towns over, near my new daughter-in-law's parents. I'd helped her decorate while Thomas was away in service, and I went there often to help Regina and tend to my first grandchild.

I had called Thomas in a panic earlier that evening. Mercy's car keys were here. But she was gone. We drove around and did not see Mercy anywhere, not even at her favorite hangout spots. We were praying that she was with Thomas and his family. When we called Thomas, he was calm and so sure she would turn up soon. But he admitted he had not seen or heard from her. He had not even told her he was in town. I never knew when he came over. But I was so grateful he did. "I'm sure your wife is mad we pulled you away for this nonsense," I said to him.

"It's ok. She is a little worried too. But she is sure Mercy is fine, just a little teenage rebellion that she trusts you to rebuke out." We laughed again. "Mercy is okay, right, Mom?" he asked.

"Yes. Yes, she is okay, sorry. She is with Auntie Kemi, of all people, I just…" I fought back tears. Thomas sat quietly beside me. "You're a good mom," he comforted me. "In fact, a great one," he went on. "The only thing is that…. well, if there is one thing you can do better…"

"Well, go on. Don't hold back now, Mr."

"Well, I wish you would talk to us more." Is that all he had to say? "Thomas, I talk to you guys all the time. You don't listen!"

"No. Mom we do listen. But it's hard to listen to what you don't say." He had my attention now. "You tell us these general things and you brag about how far God brought you. But you don't really share the stuff that maybe we can relate to. It's like you don't want us to pity you or see you as anything other than this strong Nigerian woman who made it out of the gutter. But, you don't tell us about the gutter. It's like you were never scared or afraid. Just perfect," he explained.

"I share with you, but there are some things that are personal and that I want to protect you from."

"But that's the thing, Mom. Protect us from what? What happened to you? What hurt you that you think you have to be so hard on us? I am not saying you're wrong. As you can see, I am finishing my degree now, finally on my own, without you pressuring me. I am doing well, though maybe I did take the long way- but it's all because you helped me. But maybe I would have listened quicker if you just kept it real with me from the beginning. Maybe Mercy will listen, too." I didn't know what to say. "Mom, when I was younger… before you remarried Dad, I would be in the other room, and sometimes, I would hear you crying. I don't know if you knew, but sometimes, I heard your prayers too. The ones for Daddy and others, I didn't really understand because I was so young. But even when I got older, I wondered. But you never told me and I didn't know if I could ask. Well, I am a dad, now. So, I am asking for the sake of my child. What did you go through? Help me see the world through your eyes. Please, Mom."

I was speechless, he was getting too close. How would giving him the disgusting details of my past life help him to be a better father?

"Son, you will be a great dad. You are a great dad. It's good that I never exposed you to the negative parts of my life. What good would it do to you?" He looked disappointed but I continued on. "You finally listened to me in the end, right?"

"Yah, but not without making so many mistakes that could have been avoided. Mom, you always tell us to be honest with you but if there's things about your life you have to keep hidden, are you being honest with yourself?"

He was cutting it way too close. "I really appreciate you being here, Thomas. Your dad and I are so proud of you, but I think your wife will want you home. It's very late, in fact, it's early the next day and I don't want you with this habit that it's okay to be away from home at such hours of the night."

"Mom, you can't be serious, we are having a talk."

"Thomas, go home, I mean it. I will see you in the morning. Dad and I will update you and Regina about Mercy."

"Mom!"

"Kiss my grandbaby, I need to go pray and sleep." I finished my water and gave Thomas a kiss on the forehead. "Please lock the door on your way out." With that, I went downstairs to my secret place. I heard my front door slam on my way down.

IX.

THROUGH A MIRROR DARKLY

In my secret place stands a mirror, a mirror I owned for many years. It's the same mirror I kept when Thomas was just a little boy, and it was just he and I. Sometimes, when I talked to God I stood there before it, to try to see what He saw in me. To this day, I honestly don't know.

The mirror was a gift to me. I finally decided to get my life right before God. I'd made a vow to Him that if He would deliver me from the hell I was in… the abuse, the shame, the let downs from men, that I would serve Him all the days of my life. I told Him that I would come to Him alone for peace and not turn to a bottle of wine or anything else I once used to drown my sorrows in.

He answered my prayer, and I was truly grateful. I got out of my toxic situations and eventually got my own place. The mirror was one of the first "housewarming" gifts I received for my new apartment. It was a gift from one of the ministers at my church and it marked a new season in my life. Of course, even God delivering me from such heartbreak and shame did not take all my pain away. I would go to church Sunday after Sunday and even during the week, yet I still wasn't healed. I still was not whole. So much of what I had gone through had broken me. Or so I once thought.

Years ago, I stood before that mirror lonely and crying out. I wanted to do the same thing today. I had in my mind that my worst fears were about to come to pass right before my eyes. I wanted to come to God angry and crying, but instead, all I could do was give God glory. As He always did, the devil told me I was alone, that I had messed up and driven the people I cared about away. But I knew I was no longer alone. I had my beautiful family- the family I prayed for and was proud of. I had my church family. I had God Almighty by side.

My son, like his father, so full of wisdom. My husband, like our Heavenly Father, so patient and kind. I never knew what it was about me that God would think I deserved such a gift. But I was grateful He did.

What about your daughter? She's gone. All alone in the world, just like you were. People will take advantage of her. She will end up just like you. Pregnant. Alone. Unloved. Rejected and lied to. Hurt and talked about. The devil was such a bastard. Always talking. Always lying. *She will never forgive you. How long did it take you to forgive your mother for sending you all the way overseas alone? She didn't protect you. She couldn't. Just like you can't protect your daughter.*

I rebuked the voice at once. I don't even know why. My flesh knew Satan was right. No amount of money or status… no amount of time in the church could keep my daughter safe from the dangers that awaited her in that cold world once she made up her mind to leave. Instantly, my mind flashed back to when I made that same choice.

"Iya mi..." I greeted my mother, doing my absolute best to keep my excitement in check. Mama looked up from her work. I could see she was very busy and ordinarily she would have told us so, but she sensed it was important and gave us her curious attention. Her and Auntie exchanged greetings silently.

Finally, I could hold it in no longer. “I'm going to America. North America. I'm leaving with Auntie.” I let out a sigh of relief. It was out there now. She pushed her glasses down from her eyes to be sure of what she was hearing. Then she turned her attention directly to Auntie who stood there calmly, a subtle smile plastered on her powdered face as if we hadn't dropped any bombshell at all.

"Se looto?" she asked. Auntie's smile widened. The sun radiated through my mother's office window, leaving Auntie's unreasonably white teeth glistening.

"Bẹẹni, arabinrin mi," Auntie affirmed. They stared at each other awhile. I didn't know what to think.

“Hmm” She shook her head and smiled slightly. Her magenta lipstick glistening. “You will be the one to tell your father…” I jumped for joy... ignorant of the darkness that laid ahead.

My mom's sister came from overseas to visit us in Nigeria. I had just gotten home from school. I hated boarding school. The seniors were so mean to me. They were horrible. I would have given anything to go to regular day school so I could be home. But my brothers were home to pick on me too. I could not win, either way. My parents loved me. Daddy even spoiled me if I was being truthful, but my brothers could not stand me for that. I really was like Joseph. I kept my head up, but I always felt like the odd one out.

It was not a holiday, but I came home to get money for my school fees and because I heard my auntie was visiting. I was so happy to see her. She lived the most amazing life overseas.

"My daughter, how are you doing?" she asked me. "I'm okay, Auntie."

"Are you done with school?"

"Well, almost. I have about one more test to go. It's kind of boring though. The work is very easy." My auntie laughed. "And how are your brothers treating you when you're home? You will be home to stay soon with one more school term to go." I rolled my eyes. "You know, Auntie, boys will be boys. Mommy and Daddy spoil them, of course." I looked down to the ground.

"Let's go out for a walk," she said.

"Okay, Auntie." I was happy. I knew when we went walking, we would stop by the market, and she would buy me something. I had my eye on one particular wrapper. As we were walking, my auntie said something that caught me completely off guard. "You should come and finish your school overseas with me."

"You mean come to Canada… and live with you?"

My auntie smiled. "…And your uncle and cousins. We would be happy to have you. And it would be good for you to see the world outside of Lagos." Her walking me into that Canadian embassy was better than any wrapper she could have bought me.

Once I got my parents approval, we moved full speed ahead. Back then, it was so easy to walk into the embassy to obtain a visa. I snatched the passport, and, in a few days, I went back to school to write my last exam. I finished high school at the age of 14. I was ready to go.

I never knew how much pain awaited me on the other side. *And that's what you want for your daughter, right? She is so happy to be with her aunt. Only God knows the mischief she will get into with those other girls she calls cousins. One of them looks pregnant already. They will use her like they used you.*

I closed my ears to the devil and opened my mouth and began to speak in other tongues. I called out every covenant promise of God I could think of, to counter the lies I was hearing from the devil. I casted out every fear. Satan would not have my child. Nor would I go crazy with fear and worry. The Lord brought what my son Thomas said to my mind. I remember what Daniel told me also. They were right. There was so much we did not talk about. Because we wanted to protect them. I heard the voice of the Lord, as plain as day. *"We overcome by the blood of the Lamb and the Word of our testimony."* Silence would not protect my children. But my testimony would. *Now is the time,* I heard the voice of the Lord say.

I began to worship the Lord and as I did, I received instruction. I did not know if the instruction meant I would get my daughter back, but I knew that instruction would enable me to do what I had never been able to do before: surrender her and all my children totally unto the Lord God Almighty, trusting that He will keep them in perfect peace.

X.

THROUGH HER EYES

I was extremely skeptical when my Auntie told me Mommy was coming over. I thought about skipping out. I could go to Jeremy's house or back to Anjoli's. Anywhere but here. I didn't have time for her silly, selfish lectures about how she was such a righteous victim. I just wanted to be free- to live my life.

I thought about Anjoli and what she told me about her family. It sent chills down my spine. Was I being selfish? Was I ungrateful? No. I just wanted to be free. I also did not want to feel so alone. "You understand, right, God?" It's not like I wanted to live a life of crime.

Maybe I had overreacted. But my mother still needed to learn. She can't control everything. I made up my mind that I was not going back home. I would get a job and finish school and go to college. I would emancipate myself completely and be free of all the pressure. Learn to live life on my terms. Like Thomas and Anjoli. Just then, I heard the doorbell ring. *Mom*, I thought. *It must be her… and so soon.* I truly was not ready, but I knew I did not have a choice.

"Mercy!" my Auntie called. "You have a visitor." I suddenly felt sick. I took a deep breath and mustered up the courage. I would tell my mother, today. My word would be final. I took one more deep breath and headed downstairs to the living room. It was not my mother. It was my brother, Thomas. "Thomas?" I asked, surprised. You're in town? What are you doing here? And congrats on my new niece. She looks just like me!" I gave Thomas the biggest hug, still confused about why he was here. He must have gotten leave to see his baby.

"I'm here to talk to you."

I rolled my eyes. "Mom called you," I stated.

"…And Dad called me too," he told me. I sighed as we sat on the couch. Auntie bought us orange juice and a tray of fruit. "Thank you, Auntie," we both said in unison. We laughed.

"You and me, we are a lot alike, sis."

"I guess. But I'm better looking."

"Whatever," he grinned.

Suddenly everything I'd found in the garage came to my mind. "Thomas, I know you came to do Mom's bidding, but the truth is there is a lot you don't know."

"Oh yeah? Try me." He sat back as if he knew everything I was going to say. "Well, even if you do know, Mom is a liar. Why did she keep all this from us. From you? I can't imagine how you felt when you found out Dad was not your real dad."

"Easy, Sherlock. I knew all along."

"Well … do you even know who your real dad is?"

"Yes, I talk to him from time to time as well," he stated calmly.

"Wow! Well, do you know about all Mom's abortions. She is such a saint but if you saw what I saw… I wonder who their dads were. And can you believe I had a twin? I am a twin. I was not supposed to be alone in this world!"

"Mercy, what makes you think you were ever alone?" I did not answer him. He wouldn't understand. He kept on talking. "You think God was not with you all those times in the hospital keeping you alive? You don't think Mom and Dad and the church members and angels were always there, right by your side?" Still, I had no response. "Mercy, I'm sorry to say, but you are a bit spoiled."

"Ahh! Me? Spoiled?"

Look who was talking. The only person more spoiled than him was Daniel.

"Mercy, you think the entire world revolves around you. It was me and Daniel who were always home alone while Mom attended to you. It was you they were always praying for. You got all the attention. You got all your healing and still you want to talk about being lonely. You never think about how everybody else was doing or what we missed out on or what we were going through."

I was speechless.

"I am not saying this to make you feel bad. I am just talking so you will open your eyes. Everybody is going through one thing or the other. Learn to see things through someone else's for once. Do you even try to see things from Mom's perspective. I understand she is a bit much, but do you ever think about why? Do you even ask, except to complain about not getting your way? At some point, you do have to grow up. You are not a baby or a victim of circumstances anymore. It is time to make choices and take responsibility, stop blaming everything on a sickness you don't even have any more." I began to cry. His words stung me badly. Mainly because they were true.

"I know you know Mom is on her way here," he went on. "Please, just try to listen for once. At least try. See things from her perspective, then talk. It is taking a lot for her to come here and meet you on your terms when it's really you that should go home begging after sneaking out the house and running away and all that. Please don't take it for granted." My eyes were glued to the ground. "Please promise you will listen, okay?" He asked me a final time. Tears were still flowing from my down casted eyes as he awaited my response. "Fine. I'll try," I mustered. We sat together, quietly on the couch until Mom came.

Mom came a few minutes later with Daniel and Dad. They greeted. Auntie had sent her daughters on errand to give us privacy. Once we all sat down, Daddy prayed. I had not made eye contact with anyone before then. I had no idea where this meeting was headed. I knew I would be painted the bad guy. The one at fault. Maybe I was. But it was not without good reason, and I was ready to let them have it. After Daddy prayed, the mood was calm, and Mom began to speak. I braced myself, but all I heard was stories… and I began to see them. As she talked, I saw her like I'd never seen her before. She was both weak and strong at various points throughout the stories. Some of what she shared made me cringe. Out of the corner of my eye, my auntie was there, struggling not to shed a tear.

My dad sat strongly by her side. I could tell he heard it all before, but he treated it so delicately, like he knew how hard it was for her to talk.

"It was the most anxious time for me. I never knew what was up ahead. The thoughts. The awkwardness. The fear of judgment and wasted time. I had this… 'Do they even want me here feeling?' and I would be thinking, like... am I even supposed to be here?" Mommy continued her story, tearing up in a way I had never seen up close before. But she pushed through her tears to finish her story. "The regret... I never felt so rejected." Then she looked directly at me. "I just didn't want that for you, Mercy. You are my only daughter, and I was so blessed that God chose me of all people to be your mother, the miracle you are. And I always feared that I will pass all my mistakes and blunders to you like a curse. I did everything in my power to hide everything negative from you, hoping and praying that you would not inherit any of my bad habits or experiences... the problems I had with men over the years. I only wanted you all to see what was good." By now, we were all in tears. I was still speechless. My mother went on.

"When you are honest, God meets you where you are and gives you answers of peace. Mercy, you are wanted. You are loved. You are accepted. You are not the status quo. You are not normal and that's okay. Step out in faith and according to the word and will of God, He will give you answers of peace. It's what He did for me, and I am telling you He is ready to give that to you. You don't have to run and search any more. The love and freedom you are looking for is here and in your reach. You just have to choose it." She smiled and caressed my cheek and I felt so loved. By her and by God and everyone He surrounded me with.

"As I got older, I realized God preserved my life and soul. Being an only daughter, I would have been spoiled. I went through a lot, but it matured me. I started out Baptist, then Pentecostal. I was at church every Sunday as little girl… I memorized Bible scriptures just like I had you all. It all stuck with me for when I would need it. Everything, the good and bad worked in my favor. The same will happen for all of you in Jesus' mighty name." We all said 'Amen'.

EPILOGUE

"I never got to tell Mama off, the way I originally planned." Isabel looked broken hearted, as if that was the main part she was waiting for. Knowing her, it's all she wanted to hear. She wanted me to validate what was on her stubborn little mind. She let out a sigh of disappointment.

"Well, did she let you stay with your auntie like you wanted?" I laughed.

"Izzy, is that all you got from this story?"

"Auntie, I want to stay with you! At least, just for my birthday weekend. Please! Mommy is mean and all Daddy does is pray and talk quietly all the time, quoting stuff from the Bible."

All I could do was laugh. *This girl will not kill me today,* I thought to myself. "Well, he gets that from our father," I responded, still chuckling to myself. Isabel rolled her eyes. She was the sassiest eleven-year-old I'd ever met. I wondered where she got it from. "Auntie, I am almost twelve. I just want to do what all the other almost twelve-year-old girls get to do. I just want a little freedom, you know? A little normal fun. It's weird having a Nigerian dad and an American mom who go to church all day every other day. I just want to be normal."

I smiled.

She went on. "I bet you're gonna let your baby have a normal life, right?" she asked, pointing to my giant belly.

"Nope. Because my baby will not be normal, just like you are not normal. You guys are special. You live under a special covenant and the sooner you embrace that, the easier your life will be," I counseled as I looked into her eyes.

"Trust me."

THE END